Listen to Your Heart

BECKY HARMON

BELLA
B O O K S

2018

Bella Books, Inc.
P.O. Box 10543
Tallahassee, FL 32302

Printed in the United States of America on acid-free paper.

First Bella Books Edition 2018

Editor: Medora MacDougall
Cover Designer: Judith Fellows

ISBN: 978-1-59493-594-7

Other Bella Books by Becky Harmon

Tangled Mark
New Additions
Illegal Contact

Acknowledgments

As always my first thanks has to go to Linda and Jessica Hill. Without them there would be no Bella Books. I love my Bella family. Each and every author at Bella makes us better and better.

A big thanks has to go to all the folks that work behind the scenes at Bella. The amount of work that goes into creating each title is mind-blowing and you guys do it to perfection. And, of course, a big thanks to Kathy for another perfect title.

To Medora MacDougall, editor extraordinaire, you continually amaze me. Your encouragement and knowledge bring out the best in every story you touch. Thank you for making this book another one we can both be proud of.

Thank you, Judy Fellows, for making the cover reflect an insight to the story behind it. The cover is the first thing everyone sees and you always make us look good.

The biggest thanks goes out to all the readers who take a chance each time they pick up one of my titles. Without you, I would be only entertaining myself and that would be very lonely.

About the Author

Becky Harmon was born and raised just south of the Mason-Dixon Line. Though she considers herself to be a Northerner, she moved south in search of warmth. Romance has always been her first love, and when she's not writing it, she's reading it. Her previously published works, *Tangled Mark*, *New Additions*, and *Illegal Contact*, are available from Bella Books. You can reach Becky at beckyharmon2015@yahoo.com.

Dedication

For DB
I'm listening to my heart

CHAPTER ONE

Deputy Steph Williams unsnapped the holster on her hip as she slid from the Berkeley County Sheriff's Department cruiser. Using her flashlight, she peered into the windows of the empty car, looking for any identification or illegal items. The black Mercedes with Tennessee plates was too nice to have been abandoned, but she didn't see any obvious signs that it was disabled. The radio at her belt crackled as the dispatcher identified the owner of the vehicle.

"Jemini Rivers." Steph shook her head, repeating the name through gritted teeth and lamenting her decision to help out a coworker by working uniformed patrol. She wouldn't have thought that Jemini would have the courage to return to Riverview, but apparently money still spoke to some people. It had been barely two weeks since Dorothy Rivers had passed away, and Steph's anger at Jemini for never visiting her aging grandmother was stronger than ever. She slapped the roof of the car, reminding herself that it was her responsibility nevertheless to make sure she was not in danger. "Talk about no good deed going unpunished."

After making sure the Mercedes was secure, she returned to her cruiser. The closest town, Riverview, was several miles away. It seemed unlikely Jemini would have walked in that direction. Steph was fairly sure she knew where she would find her. Clearing the scene with dispatch, she made a U-turn and headed for Lake View Resort. The entrance gate there was secured at dark, but she knew the owner, Cassie Thomas, wouldn't turn away a stranded traveler especially if she had an empty cabin.

Steph shoved the turn signal a little harder than necessary as she slowed at the entrance to the resort. Her grip on the steering wheel tightened as she thought about coming face-to-face with Jemini Rivers. Each year on Dorothy's birthday, Steph had begged her to go to dinner or a movie, but Dorothy had always refused. Instead they sat on the porch and waited for her granddaughter to visit. She never came, shattering Dorothy's heart on more occasions than Steph could count and leaving her to try to ease the disappointment of her neighbor and surrogate grandmother. She pushed her anger and frustration to the back of her mind. Tonight, she needed to do her job. Later she could replay the emotional turmoil of the last twenty years.

* * *

Jemini entered the Lake View Resort office and smiled at the woman behind the counter. Her shoulder-length, light brown hair was pulled away from her face with a barrette on each side. Clad comfortably in casual gray sweatpants and a rumpled blue T-shirt, she looked like she had been settled in for the evening. Jemini felt bad for disturbing her.

"Thank you so much. I wasn't sure what to do. My cell phone battery was dead, and I didn't realize I was traveling without the charger until my car died. I wasn't sure how far I was from town, but I knew it was an easy walk back to your entrance."

"No problem." The woman smiled. "I'm Kathleen. We're happy to help and we have an empty cabin. Just fill this out and we'll get you settled in. I can call my son, Greg, to pick up your car in the morning. He works at the repair shop in town."

"That would be great," Jemini said as she took the pen Kathleen offered and quickly filled in the registration form. She had been relieved to see the speaker box hanging beside the locked gate when she arrived at the entrance to the resort. Although she made several early morning visits to the gym each week, she was fairly sure Riverview was farther than she would have liked to walk in the dark.

Handing Kathleen the form and her credit card, she glanced around the small office. Two large cushioned chairs sat facing each other in the corner, and a Keurig coffeemaker with several racks of refills held the place of honor in the opposite corner. Adorning the walls were beach and forest photos framed in chestnut wood to match the office counter.

"Cassie should be finished with your cabin. Here's your key." Kathleen pointed out the window away from the main road. "Your cabin is the second one on the right. Make yourself at home and call us if you need anything."

"Great! Thanks, again." She stepped onto the porch and closed the office door behind her. Turning at the sound of an approaching vehicle, she was surprised to find a sheriff's department cruiser pulling to a stop in front of her.

The attractive woman who stepped from the cruiser was even more surprising, stopping Jemini in her tracks. Blond hair pulled back in a tight ponytail revealed high cheekbones and expressive blue eyes. As she stepped into the light spilling out from the office, her eyes settled on Jemini and their coldness penetrated her to the core. Jemini kept her voice friendly, even though it was hard not to feel wary at the reaction she was getting.

"Good evening, Deputy."

"Ms. Rivers?"

"Yes, I am. Is something wrong?"

Startled by the flash of anger in the deputy's eyes, she forced herself to wait for a response to her question, her mind racing to find an explanation for the hostility. She knew she hadn't done anything wrong, not that that was always enough nowadays.

The deputy's voice cracked as she spoke. "I found your car."

"O-kay." Jemini broke the word into several syllables, almost making it a question. She wasn't sure if she should continue talking, but it seemed like the deputy was waiting for an explanation. "The engine died. I had to leave it. I've already arranged for it to be towed first thing in the morning."

"But why are you here?" the deputy demanded.

"What?" Frowning, she took a step closer to the uniformed woman. Could she possibly not have heard her explanation? "My car broke down. I'll have it towed in the morning."

The hum of a golf cart interrupted their conversation as it pulled to a stop in front them. The woman driving it was dressed comfortably, like Kathleen inside, wearing sweatpants and a T-shirt. The only inconsistency was her left foot resting loosely on the edge of the cart, which was covered in brown work boots. Her dark hair hung just above her shoulders, moving when she did. It was parted on the side and fell across her eyes as she studied them.

"Hi. I'm Cassie," the woman said with a soft friendly voice, giving the deputy a strange look before asking. "Is everything okay?"

Jemini was relieved to see the harshness fade from the deputy's face as her gaze focused on Cassie. She left the officer to answer the question. She wasn't sure if everything was okay or not.

"Sure, everything's fine," the deputy said gruffly.

Cassie still seemed unsure; she gave the deputy a frown. "Hang out for a minute. I'm going to run Ms. Rivers over to her cabin and then I'll be right back."

Jemini studied the deputy's face to see if she would stop her from leaving. When there was no movement, she quickly climbed into the golf cart. Leaving this woman's presence seemed like a good idea, especially since she didn't know what she had done to get her so riled up.

As soon as the cart pulled to a stop, Jemini stepped out. Turning, she pulled her briefcase and overnight bag from behind the seat and slowly met Cassie's curious gaze.

"Thank you for the ride and the room," she said. She hoped she didn't sound dismissive, but she really wanted to be alone.

She was confused by the unpleasant interaction with the deputy, and she didn't expect Cassie to be able to clear things up.

"You're welcome," Cassie said hesitantly. "Is everything okay?"

"Of course."

"I got the feeling I interrupted something. Did Steph upset you?"

"Steph?" Jemini's heart stopped. *Stephanie? It couldn't be.*

"Deputy Williams."

Stephanie Williams. "Oh, right," Jemini spoke quickly, covering her shock. "She was just asking about my car."

She turned away from Cassie and climbed the stairs to the cabin. She couldn't think with Cassie's inquisitive stare on her. Although thinking was the last thing she wanted to do at the moment. She'd barely arrived in Riverview, and she was already coming face-to-face with her past. Based on the reception she had received from Stephanie it was not going to be a pleasant homecoming.

Remembering her manners, she turned after unlocking the door. "Thank you again. Good night." Without waiting for a response, she closed the door and rested her head against it. Coming here had definitely been a mistake. With or without her car, she was leaving Riverview tomorrow.

* * *

Resting her head in her hands, Steph closed her eyes. This wasn't the way she had imagined a meeting going between her and Jemini. She knew their childhood friendship was a thing of the past, but she would never have guessed that she would have trouble forming a sentence in her presence. After all, for twenty years she had been imagining all the things she would say to Jemini if she ever had the chance.

No, things certainly had not gone the way she had planned. She had definitely not been prepared for the beautiful woman she had found herself standing face-to-face with. Jemini wasn't the horrible monster she had always imagined she would be. The blue suit she wore looked freshly pressed despite the late hour and had been cut to mold the curves of her body. Short dark hair framed her face, setting off deep brown eyes that were several shades darker than her mocha skin.

Steph remembered those eyes. Even as a child they could stop adults in their tracks. Steph had jokingly referred to it as her "lawyer look." It was the look Jemini said she planned to use on opposing counsel when she became a famous attorney. Though Elaine Jones, a civil rights activist, was the hero Jemini's mother had chosen for her to follow, it was really actress Phylicia Rashad, from an 80s television sitcom, who taught Jemini her look. Seeing Jemini now, Steph had no problem believing Jemini must have fulfilled her dream.

In a flash, her anger was back, roaring in her ears. She fought the urge to go after Jemini and demand answers. She was so alive and vibrant and Dorothy was gone. It felt so unfair. Taking a deep breath, she stretched her legs out in front of her body. She watched the headlights on the golf cart as it came back toward her and she knew she had two choices: confess her feelings to the driver or leave. Cassie Thomas had already read more in her face than she would have liked to reveal. A one-time girlfriend, Cassie was now her best friend.

"All right, spill it," Cassie said with a nudge as she dropped down beside her on the steps.

"Spill what?"

"Let's start with the look on your face and what it has to do with that woman."

Steph shrugged and stood. "I should get back to work."

"Wait a minute." Cassie stood too. "We haven't talked in weeks and you're not going to blow me off. What's going on with you? Do you know that woman?"

"No, I don't know her. Not really anyway."

"What's that mean?"

"She's Dorothy's granddaughter."

Cassie sank back down onto the steps. "Oh, wow."

"Yeah." Steph dropped beside her with a sigh. "Wow is right."

"What's she doing here?"

"I asked her the same question, but she didn't answer. I guess she's here for the reading of the will."

"That's tomorrow afternoon, right?"

"Yeah, at three."

They sat in silence as the frogs around the nearby lake chirped their nightly tune. Her frustration faded with each moment that passed. She didn't know how long it would take to get over her sadness at the loss of Dorothy, but she did know seeing Jemini again wasn't helping.

After a while, Cassie spoke softly, "Did you know she was so beautiful?"

Steph shook her head. "She's always been an ogre in my mind. Maybe with a few horns."

"And several extra eyes."

Their laughter died as the door opened behind them. Kathleen stepped onto the porch and handed each of them a mug of tea. "Hey, Steph," she said as she ran her hand through the hair on Cassie's head.

Cassie stood. "Are you going to bed?"

"I am." Kathleen leaned in for a kiss. "Good night, Steph. It's good to see you. Come by on Friday for the cookout if you can."

Steph watched the sappy look Cassie gave Kathleen as she disappeared back inside. She had never seen her this happy. The emptiness she felt at that realization surprised her. Two children, Greg and Chase, and a girlfriend had given Cassie an instant family. She didn't want her life to be as complicated as Cassie's had become as a result. She had always liked being alone, but lately…

Cassie took a sip of her tea before speaking. "You should come Friday night."

"I'll think about it." Steph crossed to her cruiser and poured the tea into her travel mug. "You should get inside before Kathleen goes to bed without you."

Cassie smiled. "Yeah, I'm pretty lucky."

"Thrown into family life? I'm not sure I'd call that lucky."

She ducked her head, feeling her ears heat with embarrassment. The words she'd uttered sounded harsh, even to her own ears. She did believe Cassie was lucky to have Kathleen. But that didn't mean her own life was missing something. She hated the maxim that everyone needed someone to complete them. She didn't. Well, she was pretty sure she didn't.

"Greg stays at a friend's in town most nights, so only Chase is here. It's been so perfect I have to believe it was meant to be."

"Just keep telling yourself that," Steph joked, making sure her quip sounded light this time and ignoring the twinge of loneliness she felt at the thought of returning to her own empty house.

Cassie smiled. "So, we'll see you Friday night then."

Handing her empty mug to Cassie, Steph rolled her eyes. "I'll call you."

* * *

Cassie watched Steph's cruiser disappear down the driveway before stepping inside and turning out the lights. She locked the front door and climbed the stairs. In the glow from the hallway nightlight she gently pushed open Chase's bedroom door and stepped inside. His thin frame was barely visible under the covers. He had grown so much in the last nine months, it was impossible to keep any weight on him. She brushed the hair out of his eyes and kissed his forehead. She gave a whispered thanks for his health and happiness before closing his door enough to block out most of the light from the hallway.

She stepped into the bedroom she shared with Kathleen and smiled as Kathleen glanced up from her book.

"Steph okay?" Kathleen asked.

"I guess. She's in for a rough couple of days though."

"Things weren't rough already?"

She pulled her shirt over her head and tossed her remaining clothes into the laundry basket. Lifting the covers, she slid naked into the bed. Kathleen closed her book and laid it on the nightstand before switching off the lamp.

"What's going on?" Kathleen asked as she rolled on her side, resting her hand in the middle of Cassie's chest.

"Jemini is Dorothy's granddaughter."

"Why did she come now? Doesn't she know she missed the funeral?"

"Steph asked but didn't get an answer. It's probably been twenty years or more since they've had any contact." She sighed and kissed the top of Kathleen's head. "Jemini's mother took her away when she was a kid and she hasn't been back since."

"Do you know why?"

"No. Steph never knew. Dorothy wouldn't talk about it. Every year Dorothy would send Jemini an invitation to visit and Steph would wait with her, but Jemini never showed. It broke Steph's heart, but Dorothy wouldn't stop sending the invitations or waiting. She believed one day Jemini would come home to Riverview."

"That's so sad."

"It is, but Steph isn't sad anymore. Now she's angry. At the funeral, she said she would throw Jemini in jail if she ever showed up in Riverview."

"Well, that didn't happen."

"Not yet."

Kathleen snuggled closer into Cassie's body. "Chase wants to go horseback riding tomorrow."

"Chase wants to go horseback riding every day."

"Yes, but tomorrow is your day to take him."

"Okay, but I'm going to need pancakes for breakfast."

Kathleen laughed. "Why are you telling me? You can make pancakes on your own."

She tightened her arms around Kathleen, her hands sliding across the smooth, familiar skin. "I'll make them, but you have to eat with us too."

"I'll have some eggs, but I can't eat the way you guys do or I'll gain forty pounds overnight."

She groaned. "Let's stop talking about food. I could eat a pancake right now, and for the record you're beautiful with or without forty pounds of pancakes."

Kathleen slid her hand across Cassie's breast. "I can distract you from food."

She pushed the covers away, giving Kathleen space to straddle her stomach. "Yes, please do." She lifted her head and met her lips.

CHAPTER TWO

Jemini pulled her only clean suit from the hanger. She hadn't packed for more than an overnight stay and she hoped her broken-down car wouldn't ruin that plan. Thankfully, the steam from the shower had helped to disperse the few remaining wrinkles in her beige pants and jacket. Her shirt was a different story, though. She located an iron in the closet and plugged it in.

Everything about the cabin had been perfect, and staying here was certainly more private than the room she had booked at The Riverview Inn would have been. Lake View Resort was definitely more pleasant than Dorothy's empty house could possibly have been as well. Not that she had even considered staying there, though the attorney had offered that option when he called to tell her about the reading of the will. She didn't need a crystal ball to understand what that invitation meant, but she couldn't figure out why Dorothy would leave anything to a granddaughter she had cast away. Apparently Dorothy hadn't been aware that Jemini had followed in her mother's footsteps, choosing an openly lesbian lifestyle instead of living a lie. No doubt she would have been banned from Dorothy's house forever just as her mother had been. Now that she knew Stephanie was still in town and, for all Jemini knew, that she still lived in the caretaker's cottage next door, she had no intention of setting foot in or near Dorothy's house.

For the last twenty years, she had avoided any reminiscing, cursing anything that reminded her of happier times in Riverview. But last night she had laid awake for hours thinking about Stephanie. The breathtaking deputy who had stepped out of the car was nothing like the angry woman Stephanie had morphed into seconds later. She had trouble even connecting the two images. Stephanie was beautiful, but that flash of hatred was not what Jemini had expected. Was Stephanie angry because she left Riverview or because she never returned? Did that mean she didn't know why Jemini's mother had been banned from Dorothy's house? Maybe she did know and, now as an adult, she agreed with Dorothy's cruel words.

As she pressed the hot iron to the wrinkles in her shirt, she remembered the day her mother told her they were leaving Riverview. She had been playing outside with Stephanie, who had returned to her own house to get lunch. When she came inside for her own lunch, her mother had their bags packed and her grandmother was nowhere in sight. As she helped her mother carry their suitcases to the car, she fired nonstop questions that only a child would be brave enough to ask. Why couldn't she say good-bye to her grandmother and Stephanie? When would she see them again? Where were they going? How long would they be gone? Why were they leaving? The years had not lessened the pain she had felt at losing her grandmother, but learning why it had happened had made it easier to never return.

She finished dressing and packed her few belongings. She didn't plan on checking out of the cabin yet, but she could always do it over the phone as long as she didn't leave anything behind. She stepped onto the porch and closed the door behind her. The coolness of the air-conditioned room faded quickly in the morning humidity. One more reason to dislike being back in Florida. The woman who had checked her in the night before stopped as she passed the cabin.

"Good morning, Ms. Rivers."

"Good morning. Kathleen, right?" She was thankful the name had come quickly to her mind.

"Right." Kathleen smiled. "I'm taking my morning walk. Would you like to join me? Greg just called to say it'll be about fifteen minutes before he gets here with your rental car."

Jemini had never been a fan of one-on-one conversations. Small social interactions made her palms sweat. She preferred to speak in courtrooms where her script was already written, like an actor performing in front of her audience. She was unable to think of a reason not to walk with Kathleen, however, and she didn't want to be rude. She left her bags on the porch and joined her in the driveway. They crossed to the sidewalk that circled the lake and immediately fell into a relaxed pace.

The lake and surrounding pastures were quiet and peaceful. The only sounds were the chirping of birds and the splashing of water on the lake. The large fountain in its center pushed the water away, causing ripples to cascade to the shoreline on all sides. The path around the water was wide enough for the two of them to walk side by side. Park benches and old-fashioned light posts lined the walkway and she wondered why she hadn't noticed them last night. She could imagine how pretty it was in the dark. As they passed the empty swimming area, she could see the floating dock anchored not too far from the sandy beach.

"It's so peaceful here," she said, breaking the comfortable silence that had developed between them.

Kathleen chuckled. "I thought that too when I first visited. Wait until everyone wakes up and things pick up. No large families, though, this week, so you won't have the screaming of children to enjoy. Are you visiting or passing through?"

This was what Jemini hated most about one-on-one conversations. She resisted the urge to be short with her answer. "I have business in Riverview."

"What business are you in?"

"I'm an attorney, but my business here is personal not professional."

She braced herself for the normal follow-up question but was pleasantly surprised when Kathleen veered in another direction.

"Will you be staying until Friday?"

"I'm not sure. It depends on what happens at my meeting this afternoon." She cringed as she remembered the dead battery on her phone. "And if I can find a charger for my phone. It's bad enough being away from my office, but I can't be unreachable."

Kathleen nodded. "You're welcome to use our phone in the office, and if you decide to stay until Friday, you'll have to come to our cookout. Most of our other guests will attend and sometimes a few friends wander by. In fact, Cassie said she invited Steph. She's the deputy you met last night."

Jemini could feel Kathleen's eyes on her and she fought to keep the heat from her face. *Stephanie again.* After last night's reception, she was fairly sure a friend of Stephanie's was not going to be friend of hers. She had really enjoyed the walk and conversation, but she should probably leave before her real reason for being in Riverview was revealed.

"I don't think I'll still be here on Friday, but thank you for the invitation."

She was glad Kathleen didn't force conversation to fill the silence between them. With only the occasional sounds from the awakening guests, she was able to appreciate the beauty of the lake and the tree-lined pasture. She considered for a moment the idea that she might want to stay another night. Disappearing into the forest on one of the many trails seemed like a great way to spend the day. The low heels she wore rubbed her feet, reminding her she wasn't really dressed for a day of relaxation.

As they rounded the end of the lake again and headed back toward the office, a black Toyota Camry pulled to a stop in front of them. A tall, lanky teenager climbed from behind the wheel. His jeans were faded and marked with a few permanent grease stains as was the T-shirt that hung from his shoulders. The smile on his face was huge as he stepped toward them.

"Hey, Greg." Kathleen gave him a quick hug before turning to Jemini. "This is Ms. Rivers."

"It's a pleasure to meet you, ma'am." Greg shook her hand and then handed her the key to the Camry.

"Likewise," she said, passing him the key to her Mercedes.

"Jo thinks it might be the fuel pump, which would be an easy fix, but we'll know more when we get it back to the shop."

"I have a meeting at three, but I'll come by after that."

"Great. We'll see you then." He turned to Kathleen. "I better catch up with Jo before she leaves me. She'll have the car loaded on the truck by now." He gave a wave and took off at a jog.

Jemini looked at Greg's disappearing form and back to Kathleen. "I can give him a ride."

Kathleen laughed. "He's fine."

The office door opened and Cassie stepped out flanked by two black, curly-haired dogs. "Was that Greg?"

"Yes, and he's already gone."

Cassie smiled. "I swear he never stops moving."

A small boy dressed in jeans and cowboy boots stepped out of the office behind Cassie. "Did I miss Greg?"

Cassie ruffled his hair. "I'm sorry, Chase. I missed him too. Maybe after our ride we can swing into town and visit him for a minute."

"Cool and then we can get ice cream." He didn't wait for a response but called both dogs and headed for the barn. "Dillon and I will get the horses ready," he called over his shoulder.

Jemini felt like the outsider she was as she watched the two women share a look and then begin to laugh.

"I guess I better join him or he might leave without me. It was nice meeting you, Ms. Rivers."

Kathleen turned to Jemini. "I'm sorry if we were distracted by Chase. Cassie just bought him new boots and they seem to have a built-in swagger."

Jemini chuckled. "How old is he?"

"He just turned ten."

"He acts older and much more confident than most ten-year-olds."

"Thank you." Kathleen's face flushed with pride. "He was forced to grow up faster than most kids, but now he gets to be a kid again."

She wanted to ask Kathleen to explain what she meant, but she was reminded of the day she had in front of her. She wasn't here to make friends, even if she did find these two women intriguing. They were locals and she already knew they were Stephanie's friends. What was she thinking anyway? She was leaving today. "I guess I should try to find a phone charger."

"There's an electronics store beside the diner on Main Street. You can't miss it."

"Great! I'm sure I'll find it then. Thanks."

She pulled the door of the Camry shut, relieved to finally be alone. She liked Kathleen and Cassie but was a little intimidated by their friendliness and their relationship. She didn't know a lot of couples that were making it work. Most women she knew were focused on their professions and any women in their life took a backseat. Swinging by the porch of her cabin, she grabbed her overnight bag and the briefcase holding her laptop and headed into Riverview.

* * *

Steph rolled over and groaned as she caught a glimpse of the alarm clock on her nightstand. It wasn't even nine a.m. She had barely gotten three hours of sleep. When her shift ended at three, she had come straight home, but she hadn't been able to get Jemini out of her mind long enough to fall asleep. She was too awake to fall back to sleep now, and she knew there was no chance she would be able to catch a nap before her shift at five.

Tomorrow was her last day on this rotation, thank goodness. She would return then to her regular shift. That meant working whenever there was a case, but at least she could take a day off if she needed it.

She poured herself some coffee and stepped outside on the back deck. She couldn't stop herself from glancing toward the main house even though she knew Dorothy wouldn't be waiting. Dorothy had always seemed to know when she would be stepping outside with her coffee. That was one more thing Dorothy would never be able to explain now. That and the full story on why Jemini left. She always regretted not pushing her for that, but in the back of her mind, she realized, she had always thought Jemini would come back and explain everything.

Maybe she should give Jemini a chance to tell her side of the story. Her stomach churned at the thought. It was too late for Jemini to make things right. Dorothy was dead and that could not be undone no matter what she had to say.

She dumped her remaining coffee down the sink and changed into her running clothes. As had been her practice for the last week, she stopped at the main house and checked on Ms. Agnes before following the trail into the woods. Agnes Boone was in her seventies and spent most days in her rocking chair on the porch. Still vibrant enough to care for herself, she and Dorothy had shared their meals every day for over ten years. Dorothy had happily remodeled her home, making space downstairs for Agnes and upstairs for Kim and her son Brandon. Money or maybe loneliness had driven Agnes from her home and the same with Kim and Brandon. Kim was working hard to provide for her son when she lost her second job. Like Dorothy, Steph had enjoyed having a kid around again. One that wasn't her responsibility, that is. At ten, he was a handful of questions and energy, but he brought a youthful vibrancy back into the house. She would check on them this evening after they returned from work and school.

She tried to settle into the rhythmic sound of her shoes hitting the soft ground. Normally running was her key to relax, but today her mind wouldn't clear. Jemini Rivers was back in town and more beautiful than she could have imagined. She couldn't remember much about Jemini's appearance as a kid other than her eyes. She remembered, though, that Jemini didn't mind touching bugs or relocating spiders from their clubhouse and that she was always the one to put the bait on their hooks when they went fishing. Granted there weren't any fish in the small stream so neither had had to touch a fish, but she knew if there had been it would have been Jemini who did so.

She slowed her pace as she approached the portion of the trail that crossed the main road. Hearing the hum of a slow-moving vehicle, she stopped, jogging in place. The trail wasn't visible from the road and she didn't want to surprise the passing driver. A mid-sized black sedan passed. She didn't get a good look at it, but she thought it might have turned onto Rivers Pass. Since she and Dorothy were the only ones who owned property on that road, she considered turning around. She wasn't even halfway to her usual turnaround point, though, and she really needed to burn off her extra energy, so she decided to continue her run. Anyone who needed to see her would have to wait or come back.

* * *

Jemini hit the brakes hard as she turned the Toyota onto Rivers Pass. She hadn't bothered to get directions to Dorothy's house before leaving Chattanooga. She had been sure she wasn't going to come here, but when she left Lake View earlier, she had felt a strange pull to see her childhood home. She didn't know if she could find it by memory or if she would even be disappointed if she couldn't. As she remembered her earlier conviction to never step in or near Dorothy's house, the sick feeling that had plagued her since the attorney's call about the will returned. The feeling she hated more than anything else in her life. The one that told her she might be making a mistake.

Apparently she remembered more than she thought or maybe the roads hadn't changed much in twenty years because she had driven straight to the dirt lane which led to Dorothy's house. The road seemed longer and the house bigger, but the flashback of memories were clear. She pulled to a stop in front of the two-story white plantation house and braced her hands on the steering wheel. The huge front porch that wrapped around both sides of the house still held Dorothy's rocking chairs. She closed her eyes, letting the pictures and sounds flood her mind, hearing Stephanie's squeals as they had raced around the house playing hide-and-seek. Stephanie's fear of bugs had kept her out of most hiding places, and finding her before she could return to base had never been a problem.

Stephanie. Steph. The anguish she had felt the day her mom took her away consumed her again and she fought back a sob. She didn't know what Stephanie had been told when her best friend left and never came back. She was sure, though, that Stephanie didn't understand that while Dorothy might have just passed away, for her that loss was twenty years old.

As a teenager, Jemini had rehearsed the words she'd say when she was old enough to return on her own. When her mother finally explained the real reason they had left, though, Jemini was old enough to know she would never be able to return.

She rubbed the moisture from her face. She didn't allow herself to cry, especially not over memories, but she could still remember what it felt like to be pulled onto Dorothy's broad lap. How everything was instantly better the second she was wrapped in her loving arms. Skinned knees, bee stings, and a variety of other kid ailments always brought snuggles and cookies. To this day, she avoided baking anything sweet in order to avoid being reminded of Dorothy and the love she had felt.

Movement behind the curtain in a downstairs window caught Jemini's eye and she quickly wiped her eyes. Who was inside Dorothy's house? Was it Stephanie? Her pulse raced at the chance to see her again, but she knew at the moment she wasn't strong enough to face her. She needed the few hours until the reading of the will to tend to the brokenness inside her. Throwing the car in reverse, she turned around and headed for Riverview.

* * *

"Steph."

Steph glanced onto the porch encircling the plantation house. Agnes sat in her favorite rocking chair. Steph hesitated, waiting for Dorothy to join them, before remembering that Dorothy's memory would be the only thing joining them ever again. The two elderly women would never rock together again while Dorothy waited for whatever needed to be removed from the oven. She searched Agnes's face for signs of the pain she must be feeling.

"Everything okay?" she asked, hesitating in front of Dorothy's chair and then dropping onto the porch steps.

"Oh, child. Come up here with me. Dorothy would want you to sit in her chair."

"Not yet, Ms. Agnes. I just can't do it yet." She rubbed her face to clear the memories. "Is everything okay? Did you need something?"

Already lost again in her own thoughts, Agnes continued to rock.

Steph watched her. Agnes was only a year or so younger than Dorothy. She couldn't help to wonder if she would soon have to say good-bye to her too.

Agnes finally spoke. "There was a car earlier."

"Where?"

"It pulled up to the house and then just sat there. I hurried inside when I heard it and then was afraid to go back out when they didn't show themselves. I watched from inside the house until they left."

"That's always the best idea when you aren't sure who's out there. Could you tell what kind of car it was?"

"It was black."

Steph nodded. Apparently that was an adequate description as far as Agnes was concerned. "Did it have two or four doors?"

"It had four. I'm sure 'cause I remember thinking it looked like Kim's car, except it was black."

Steph remembered the black sedan she had passed on the road, which had indeed looked like Kim's Honda Accord. Now she wished she had turned around and returned. She didn't like that Agnes had been worried or that someone had been snooping around.

"I'll keep an eye out for it. Try not to worry for now. It was probably a solicitor and they didn't think anyone was at home."

Agnes nodded, her chair creaking with each push of her feet.

"Are you sure you don't want to come with me to the reading of the will this afternoon?" Steph asked.

"No. No, Dorothy told me everything she needed me to know before she died. I can't imagine her written wishes will surprise me."

Steph hesitated and then took the plunge. She wished she was as confident as Agnes about knowing everything Dorothy wanted her to know. Maybe Agnes knew something about Jemini that would make things clearer. "Jemini is in town."

There was a subtle delay in Agnes's rocking before it returned to its normal pace.

Steph watched her face, but her expression remained the same. "Do you think Dorothy left the house to her?"

Agnes's eyes met hers and she nodded.

The angry fire she had been pushing away burned through her again and she jumped to her feet. "Why would Dorothy do that to us?"

"She wanted to bring Jemini home."

"This is not her home!"

Agnes shrugged. "Dorothy would tell you to listen to your heart. You know what to do."

This was the worst thing that could happen as far as she was concerned. Agnes seemed resigned to whatever the outcome of new ownership might bring, but Steph was going to put a stop to it all. She would fight.

"I need to shower, but I'll be around for another hour or so if you need anything or the car returns." She tried to keep her voice from being harsh. It wasn't Agnes's fault they were in this situation.

Agnes gazed off the porch at something only she could see as the chair continued its soothing pace.

Steph followed the path back to her cottage, looking around at the beautiful blooming flowers. Steph's father had been Dorothy's caretaker. When he passed away, her mom had continued his landscaping duties, assisted by Steph, who had moved back to the cottage to help out. She had purchased the cottage from Dorothy after her mother died. Her parents had always been fine with the rental arrangement, but Dorothy had understood that Steph needed something more permanent. She had spent countless hours keeping the yard as her parents had designed it—with the supervision, of course, of Dorothy, who had eagerly played the role of Steph's grandmother, especially after Jemini had left. Steph wished her parents were here to tell her what they could of Dorothy's secrets. She missed them all very much and couldn't remember ever feeling so alone.

As she climbed the two steps leading to her small porch, she glanced back at Dorothy's beautiful house. Dorothy had never complained about outliving her husband and her son or both of Steph's parents. In fact, she could never remember Dorothy complaining about anything. No matter the situation, Dorothy's glass was always half-full, never half-empty. Over the years, she and Dorothy had talked about everything—well, everything except why Jemini and her mother had left that day. She had tried to get Dorothy to explain what happened but eventually had given up.

Stomping through her kitchen, she realized she was angrier now than before her run. When Dorothy's attorney, Gerald Cross, had explained to her that he wouldn't be able to do an official reading of the will until all involved parties were notified, she had felt sick. Dorothy didn't have any family other than Jemini and her mother; Gerald had to be referring to them. Given the way they had left and all the years that had passed, she had been confident that neither of them would appear. She'd been wrong obviously. She wasn't surprised Dorothy had discussed her wishes with Agnes, but she wished she could have had a chance to plead her case against Dorothy leaving everything to Jemini. What would Agnes and Kim do if Jemini sold the house? She had to convince Jemini that it was the wrong thing to do.

CHAPTER THREE

Jemini unwrapped the charging cord and plugged it into her cell phone and the USB port in the car. Instantly the cell phone display lit, telling her it was charging. She dialed her office.

"Thompson, Myers and Rivers. Ms. Rivers' office, can I help you?"

"Hey, Karen. It's me."

"Where have you been? I've been calling all morning."

She was always fascinated that Karen could sound reprimanding and sweet at the same time. Her life had gotten a lot easier when she hired her as her administrative assistant. A single woman in search of a career made her the perfect person to keep Jemini's work schedule organized. She was always at the office whenever she was needed, and her efficiency kept them both looking professional and competent.

"I forgot my phone charger and I just picked up a new one," she explained.

"Are you coming back today? Judge Stevens wants to hear the Watson case on Friday. I tried to explain to him that you were out of town due to a death in the family, but he said he wouldn't have another free date for two months."

She stared out the car window, barely noticing the people passing. She had been pushing to get the Watson case before a judge for almost three weeks.

"I'll be back before the hearing. Text me the details."

"Should I email you the files too?"

"Yes, please. I'll call you after the will is read this afternoon."

"I'm really sorry about your grandmother, Jemini."

"Thanks, Karen. I'll call you later."

She ended the call and tossed the still charging phone onto the passenger seat. She was in limbo until she knew what was in the will. That and what was wrong with her car. Looking at the garage across the street, she could see her car suspended in the air, two bodies standing close together underneath it. She recognized Greg from their meeting earlier in the morning. The other set of coveralls must belong to the shop owner, Jo. Given the androgynous clothing she was wearing, it was hard to tell she was a woman, but Jemini had remembered the pronoun Greg had used.

Her stomach grumbled, reminding her she hadn't eaten yet today, and she looked around for the diner Kathleen had mentioned. She would stop and check on the car after she got something to eat. Maybe she could find a way to expedite the repairs. She didn't want to remain in Riverview a second longer than necessary.

Taking her laptop, phone, and charger, she entered the diner. Everyone glanced up when the bell over the door chimed, and she quickly searched for a secluded spot. The diner was larger than it had appeared from the street. A white counter with eight red, padded swivel chairs stretched along the center of the floor. A cash register stood in the middle where a gap in the counter allowed access to the kitchen and serving area. Wrapping around the kitchen were traditional red plastic booths with Formica tables. Both sides had an additional room blocked off in the rear with square tables and chairs. She spotted an open booth in the back corner and quickly slid onto the plastic bench.

Instantly regretting her decision to sit with her back to the wall, she tried to distract herself by turning on her computer, plugging her phone in, and then opening the menu she found tucked in the metal caddy holding condiments and napkins. She was used to the occasional look and could easily ignore them. These diners however seemed to be fascinated with her, and she met several of their stares as she glanced around the room. Their eyes seemed to be merely curious, though, not hostile. She tried to put them out of her mind by focusing on the menu. The seconds passed slowly until a shadow crossed her table. The young waitress's eyes met hers with a touch of sympathy as she set a glass of water on the table.

"What can I get for you? I mean, besides a privacy bubble."

She smiled but didn't acknowledge the attempt at humor. "Scrambled eggs with cheddar cheese and home fries, please."

"And to drink?"

"Coffee would be great."

"Coming right up. I'm Vikki, by the way, if you need anything."

Jemini's smile was appreciative when she returned quickly with her coffee. There weren't as many eyes on her now, and she gave a relieved sigh. She hated being the center of attention unless she was in the courtroom. As a young attorney, she had quickly made a name for herself. Never staying for long at any job, it was clear she had been searching for something when she joined the law offices of Thompson and Myers.

The rotating pictures on her laptop's sleep screen caught her eye and she watched the memories of her life flip by. Graduations and birthdays from years ago were a blur to her now, but the picture she loved most was the day she signed as a partner at Thompson and Myers. The smile on her mother's face was huge and she knew Aries had been proud of her. Her mother's own attempt to get a college degree had been cut short by their move to Chattanooga. Without Dorothy's monetary assistance and childcare, being a single mother took precedence.

She had lived with her mother until she graduated from college. Law school had been demanding and was followed by eighty-hour workweeks. Even though they were still in the same town, she hated to admit that she hadn't made time to visit. The move from Florida and the loss of Dorothy had scarred them both.

Looking back now, though, she could see that her mother had made bigger strides to move past the betrayal than she had. There hadn't been a large number of women moving into and eventually out of her mother's life, but with each failed relationship, she hadn't given up looking for that special someone. Soon after Jemini had graduated from law school, she had found Cindi. Their relationship had allowed Jemini to withdraw further without even realizing it.

She had always thought when things slowed down they would take the time to process through their issues, but then her mother had gotten sick. Cindi took great care of her and Jemini was left to bury her head in work. When she finally came up for air, her mother was gone and she was alone in the world. Permanent relationships had become something she wanted to avoid. Cindi would have been willing to remain a part of her life, but she knew she hadn't even tried to keep in contact with her. She barely made time for dating. Robin, her current girlfriend, if you could even call her that, didn't even know why she was in Florida. In fact, she wasn't sure she had even told her where she was going.

All this reminiscing was giving her a headache. She pulled her laptop in front of her and, seeing the available Internet access, clicked on her email. Karen had already sent the Watson file, so she quickly saved it to her hard drive. She would be able to work on it tonight wherever she was. Assuming that whatever happened at the lawyer's office this afternoon didn't derail everything.

She rubbed her aching forehead, refusing to allow herself to consider the possibilities of what Dorothy's will might contain. She knew she wouldn't have been invited to the reading if she wasn't included in the will somewhere. Dorothy hated her and her mother, though, so it was a mystery why she would include either of them in anything she had to give away. Maybe this was to be one last effort to humiliate her. Making her come back to a town where everyone probably knew why she and her mother had left. Small towns gossiped about everything and everyone.

Like all of the other diners, Jemini glanced up when the entrance bell chimed. A woman about Jemini's height slowed just inside the door while her eyes adjusted to the inside lighting. Giving a few waves around the room, she crossed straight to Jemini's table and slid into the booth opposite her.

"Thanks, Vikki." The woman barely glanced up as a coffee cup appeared on the table in front of her. Her intense gaze on Jemini, she took a sip of the coffee. "I'm Jo. Greg saw the rental and we thought you might be in here getting some breakfast. I hope you don't mind the intrusion."

Jemini reached her hand across the table. "I'm Jemini."

"Right. Right, Ms. Rivers."

Jemini froze as the room went silent. She forced her face to remain blank and resisted the urge to challenge the open stares.

Jo shrugged. "Don't mind them. They knew who you were the second you walked in the door. Small town and all."

Jemini kept her gaze on Jo. "How's my car?"

"She's going to be fine. I was able to get a new fuel pump from a parts shop in Pensacola. It's been installed and Greg's wrapping things up right now. We'll give her a test drive, too, but she'll be ready by the time you finish here."

"That's good news. I was afraid I was going to have to save the pig from the town butcher to trade for parts."

Jo laughed clearly understanding her reference to an 80s movie in which a doctor headed for a plastic surgery career in Hollywood is forced to offer his services to a small town after he takes out the judge's handmade white picket fence with his car. She paused for a second seeming to consider the suggestion. "We would never force you to stay in Riverview, but we could always use a good lawyer."

"Too many lawsuits?"

"No, too much scum leaking out of Pensacola."

"I'm mostly a child advocate these days, but I'm not against locking up the scum. I don't plan on staying, though."

Vikki slid a plate in front of Jemini. "Need anything else?"

"No, I'm fine. Thank you."

Jo waited for Vikki to drift away and then met Jemini's eyes. "It's not a bad town."

"I'm sure it's not."

Jo placed both hands on the table and slid from the booth. "I'll let you enjoy your meal. Stop by when you finish."

Jemini nodded.

Jo dropped a few bills by the cash register and was gone as fast as she had appeared. Jemini hated to admit she liked anything about this town, but Jo's easygoing manner was hard to dislike. She finished her breakfast, using her laptop to keep from being disturbed by the occasional stares still coming her way. Vikki appeared at her elbow as she was taking the last bite.

Chewing her gum at a rapid pace as if to pull every last bit of flavor from it as quickly as possible, she refilled Jemini's coffee cup and leaned close. "Would you like to move to a table in the back room since you have a couple of hours to kill?"

Jemini was past being surprised that Vikki or anyone for that matter knew her plans. Everyone in the town probably knew the will was being read today.

"I'd really appreciate that. Is it okay with your boss?" Jemini looked over Vikki's shoulder at the woman accepting money at the cash register. She wore jeans like the rest of her staff, but her upper half was covered with a multicolored scrub shirt. Jemini guessed her to be in her sixties or maybe even early seventies. Her salt-and-pepper hair was short and had the rumpled slept-on look. It would have been sexy on a thirty-year-old, but on her it was just plain cute.

"It was her idea. She thought you might feel more comfortable back there."

Jemini pulled a twenty from her bag and handed it to Vikki.

"I'll be right back with your change."

"No, keep it." Jemini stood, pulling her laptop across the bench. "I'll keep my coffee, if that's okay?"

"Of course. I'll check on you, but if you need something just flag me down."

"Thank you."

Jemini met the gaze of the woman behind the register as she turned to enter the back room. Her arms filled, she gave her a thankful smile.

* * *

Steph emerged from the steamy bathroom and stretched out naked on the bed. Though she had dried off twice already the humidity was making it hard to stay that way. She closed her eyes and tried to meditate. She had never been able to master that skill, but she needed to do something to curb her anger. Dorothy's death had been a blow to her soul, and Jemini's reappearance was threatening to push her over the edge.

She glanced around at her bedroom, taking comfort in the space she had designed. She had remodeled the house after purchasing it to make it fit more of her own style. This bedroom had been hers as a child so she wanted to keep it. Pushing out a few walls had made it large enough to be a master bedroom with space enough to add her own bathroom. That left her parents' room with a private bath for guests. She had also pushed out the wall in the third bedroom to make the living room larger. The house was exactly as she wanted it now, and even though she owned it she was still afraid of what would happen if Jemini sold Dorothy's house and the property around her.

She didn't want to be angry with Dorothy for the turmoil she was causing, but she did wish she could hear her reasons for doing this. Agnes's words about bringing Jemini home were stuck in her head and she took a deep breath. Maybe Dorothy didn't leave them at Jemini's mercy. Maybe she had left Jemini something else. Steph took this thread of hope and hung on to it tightly, letting it ease her mind. Until the attorney spoke this afternoon, she could still hope for the best.

* * *

Jemini held her breath as the conversation by the cash register drifted into the back room. She'd had a productive afternoon, thanks to Vikki and her never-ending coffee refills. She was a bit wired now, but she thought she was ready to face Stephanie again. That was until she heard her voice.

"Well, why do you think she's here?" Steph's voice was hoarse, carrying easily across the empty diner.

"I don't know, Steph, but it's just wrong. Dorothy wouldn't do something like that."

"We won't know what Dorothy would do until the attorney reads the will. You know she loved that kid and we've all seen her do crazy things where she was concerned."

"Loved that kid." Jemini couldn't believe what she was hearing and strained to hear more. *Were they talking about her? Had her grandmother loved her?*

"Well, let us know the outcome and we'll do whatever you need to help out."

"Thanks."

Jemini stared at her computer screen, waiting for the door chime to announce Stephanie's departure. She placed another twenty under the salt and pepper shakers and gathered her stuff. Vikki was taking an order and had her back to her so Jemini left without looking back. She didn't want to face anyone right now, but she wanted her car back in case she needed to leave quickly after the reading. She drove the rental across the street to Jo's shop and transferred her personal belongings back into the Mercedes.

Greg jumped to his feet as soon as she came into sight. "Ms. Rivers. She's all ready to go."

She followed him into the small office, gave him the rental keys, and paid her bill. Greg talked while they exchanged money. Thankfully he wasn't big on conversation and she was able to nod as he explained what had went wrong with her car. She wished his enthusiasm was contagious.

"Here's your keys."

"Is it okay if I leave it in your lot for a short time?"

"Oh yeah, it'll be fine where it's at."

"Thanks, Greg."

As she stepped out of the office, she felt Jo's eyes on her. She scanned the bays, locating her leaning against the fender of a car watching her. Jo seemed to blend in with the predominantly male atmosphere, fitting perfectly into a space Jemini couldn't even imagine. At first glance, she looked nothing like the person Jemini had met earlier in the diner. Her baggy, grease-stained coveralls obscured all signs of her feminine appearance except the soft features of her face. Jemini gave her a wave and Jo returned it with a smile, ducking back under the hood as Greg joined her.

Crossing the street, Jemini found herself in front of the attorney's office much more quickly than she intended. She pushed through the door and the wave of cool air made her shiver. Two couches and a desk filled the reception area. A middle-aged woman with too much makeup and horribly long, painted nails sat behind the desk, talking on the phone. She stopped in the middle of her sentence, and Jemini was left with the impression she might have been the topic of conversation. Saying her good-byes into the phone, the receptionist addressed Jemini.

"Mr. Cross will be right with you, Ms. Rivers."

Jemini nodded and took a seat on the leather couch closest to the exit. Folding her hands in her lap, she stared around the room at the photographs on the wall. They looked similar to the ones in the office at Lake View and she wondered if it was a local artist. She considered asking the receptionist, but she seemed occupied by the filing cabinet behind her desk. The office reminded her of her own; she wondered why attorneys always used dark colors and leather furniture. She imagined it could be intimidating to someone walking in for the first time as well as looking expensive and prestigious. She made a mental note to scrutinize her office when she returned and see what she could change. Not realizing she had closed her eyes, she quickly opened them to the swish of movement on the carpet in front of her.

A gray-haired African-American gentleman in a three-piece suit stood in the entrance to the hallway. "Ms. Rivers?"

"Yes." She rose to her feet.

"I'm Gerald Cross. Come on back and we'll get things started."

He had a slow gentle speech that Jemini remembered from the phone call that had brought her to this town today. His close-cut hair matched his elegant, yet relaxed persona. He continued to talk as they walked, looking over his shoulder as he led her down the hall.

"I'll need to document the reading of the will. I can either do that with a video camera or a court reporter. If you don't have a preference then I prefer to use the camera. I feel like it's less intrusive than adding another body to the room."

Jemini nodded when he glanced at her. She had a video camera wired in her office as well. It was a necessary evil in today's society and she had grown accustomed to it.

He stopped and motioned for her to step inside the room first. Her eyes were immediately drawn to Stephanie. It was slightly annoying to see her looking refreshed and comfortable in one of the two dark leather chairs in front of the huge mahogany desk. Her uniformed legs were stretched out in front of her and Jemini couldn't keep from perusing her body. When her eyes met Stephanie's eyes, though, her breath caught. They were hard and cold, making her presence in the small room a frightening and dominating one. She felt herself falter. Maybe it was the dark blue and gray uniform she was wearing? That should not have any effect on her. After all, she worked with police officers every day. She certainly wasn't willing to admit her response was due more to Stephanie than the uniform.

"Ms. Rivers." Steph acknowledged her appearance.

"Deputy."

Mr. Cross took a seat in his desk chair and started the process immediately. "I must inform you that the video recorder has been started. It's my responsibility today to read the wishes of Ms. Dorothy Rivers. Dorothy was a good friend and I am very sorry for your loss." He turned his body slightly and focused on Steph. "Stephanie, Dorothy was very concerned about how you would react today so she wanted me to speak with you first. She had the property lines expanded and you now own ten acres surrounding your house."

Jemini watched Stephanie's face as Mr. Cross read the dimensions of her new property line. If she allowed herself, she could remember all the details of the landscaper's cottage. It was her second home for the time she was at Dorothy's, and Stephanie's parents had treated her like their own child. She felt sad as she realized that Stephanie's parents must have passed away. Otherwise she was sure they would be here as well. She was surprised at the relief showing on Stephanie's face; it made her wonder what Stephanie had expected. She quickly erased her frown as Mr. Cross directed his attention to her.

"Dorothy wanted you to feel comfortable in returning home. She left the house and the remaining forty acres to you."

Unable to meet Stephanie's eyes, Jemini focused her gaze on Mr. Cross, giving him a small nod.

He continued. "Based on our conversation when I called to inform you about the reading of Dorothy's will, I took the liberty of contacting a real estate agent and the house can go on the market immediately."

"What! How could you?"

Jemini watched Stephanie swallow the rest of her words as she forced herself back into the chair. Her heart ached for the pain that flashed across Stephanie's face, but she couldn't worry about that now. She had to take care of the details so she could return home.

"I appreciate your timely response, Mr. Cross. What do I need to do before leaving town?"

"You need to meet the people you're evicting!" Steph exclaimed.

"What?" Jemini's gaze swept to Stephanie.

Mr. Cross put his hands in the air. "Stephanie."

Again, Stephanie dropped back into her chair and turned her face to the wall.

"There are several tenants living in Dorothy's house," Mr. Cross explained. "But it belongs to you now, so you're free to do as you wish. Stop by the real estate office next door and Richard will give you the papers to sign. Then it's just a waiting game until someone shows an interest."

He nodded as if dismissing her and Jemini stood. "I guess we're finished here then." She glanced at Stephanie and was shocked to see the glimmer of moisture on her cheeks before she turned her face back to the wall again. Quickly, Jemini left the office, but Stephanie's face tore at her and she paused in the hallway, listening.

"I don't understand why you wouldn't let me tell her about them." Steph's voice came out in a sob.

"I'm sorry, Steph. It's her property now. She can do whatever she wants. It's the way Dorothy wanted it."

The sound of Stephanie's sobs filled Jemini's ears as she stumbled through the receptionist's office and out the door. The light from the street blinded her and she stepped around the corner into the alley. Sucking in air, she leaned against the brick wall, resisting the urge to crumble. Even though the lawyer had suggested this was a possible outcome when he called, she was still overwhelmed by what Dorothy had done. *Why would she leave everything to me?*

The look on Stephanie's face and her apparent anguish had stunned Jemini. The vision of the grandmother she had cried for at night after her mother went to sleep swept over her, and all the pain she had felt as a kid came rushing back. She took a deep breath and braced her hands on the wall, pushing herself to her feet. Dorothy didn't want her then and she certainly would not have loved the woman she had become. She was an adult now and she didn't need the memories of something that had never been real. Whatever she thought Dorothy had meant to her before she was taken away was just a childhood fantasy.

As she had a million times over the years, she pushed her feelings into the recesses of her mind, putting her professional face in place. She stepped back into the street and located the real estate office. Richard Greene had the papers laid out and within minutes she had signed them, giving him authorization to pursue buyers for a house she didn't want. She gave him her contact information and left before the first pangs of doubt could overtake her.

CHAPTER FOUR

Jemini was surprised to find Stephanie leaning against the wall outside the real estate office when she emerged. Stephanie fell into step beside her as she walked toward Jo's to get her car.

"We need to talk," Stephanie demanded.

"I'm listening."

"How can you sell the house?" Stephanie's voice was tense. Her earlier tears replaced by a rage that was almost palpable.

"Why would I keep it?"

"Because it's the right thing to do!"

"I don't have any emotional attachment to that house."

Stephanie frowned and her voice softened. "I know that's not true."

Jemini shook her head. She was not going to allow Stephanie to play on her memories and make the small wedge of doubt grow. She needed to return to her quiet peaceful life in Chattanooga and then everything would be fine. She forced all emotion out of her voice. "I don't live here. I don't know why she left the house to me. Why don't you buy it?"

She turned and walked away. She needed distance between herself and everyone in this town. She returned to her car and even though she could see Jo watching from inside the bay, she couldn't muster the strength to even wave. Her mind struggled to lock onto one thought. There was no doubt she had to sell the house and property. What else did Stephanie expect from her? Surely she didn't think Jemini was going to pack up her life and move back to Riverview. She wouldn't be happy, and she doubted that would make Stephanie very happy either. She couldn't even imagine living next door to the attractive woman Stephanie had become while at the same time trying to ignore her angry outbursts.

As she drove toward Lake View, she couldn't help dreading the three- or four-hour drive back to Tennessee. She didn't have any reason to stay in this town another night, but she felt emotionally drained. A good night's sleep and she would be eager to drive back to her condo in Chattanooga. To return to her life and put all of this past trauma behind her.

* * *

Steph watched Jemini walk away. This cold-hearted woman was not someone she wanted to be around and yet she felt drawn to her. She didn't have the time or energy to play these games. Quickly she entered the real estate office and got the asking price from Richard. She used the several-minute walk to her accountant's office to smother her anger.

She could count on Jenna Grant to always tell her the truth. If there was any way possible for this to happen, Jenna would find it. They had graduated high school together and resumed their friendship as soon as Jenna returned from college. She might have even been Jenna's first client when she opened her accounting firm. Jenna's dark hair and eyes made her look older than her years and she had a way of making Steph always think longer and harder about every financial step she took.

Jenna looked up from her desk as Steph stepped inside. "I thought I might see you today."

Steph shrugged. "I'm not sure what else to do. I can't risk Agnes or Kim and Brandon being evicted."

"You don't know what the new buyer would do."

"No, I don't, but you know as well as I do that anyone purchasing it would be looking for an investment and I'm sure they wouldn't be happy with the amount of rent either of them pay."

Jenna nodded. "Take a seat. I glanced through your file this morning. Most of the money your parents left you went to paying off the house loan. Depending on what Ms. Rivers is asking for Dorothy's property, you might be able to come up with a down payment."

Steph gave her the figure she had gotten from Richard.

"I guess that's a fair amount for fifty acres and the house, but it's more than you can afford."

"Forty acres," Steph corrected her.

Jenna raised an eyebrow.

"Dorothy left me ten acres surrounding the cottage."

"Do you think Ms. Rivers would consider selling you just the house?"

"We're not exactly the best of friends, so let's just say no."

"Okay, then. I have to advise you that this would be a poor investment that I'm not sure you have the money for anyway."

"I really don't see a choice." Steph groaned, collapsing against the back of the chair.

"Go apply for the loan, then. I'll see if I can move enough money around for your down payment."

Steph stood. "Thanks, Jenna. I owe you."

"Dinner. You can pay me with dinner."

Steph walked back to her truck and drove the short distance to the bank. As she filled out each page of the loan paperwork her anger slowly dissipated into despair. Jemini had no idea what she was asking her to do. Her sheriff's department income would barely cover a mortgage for the amount Jemini was asking and she knew it. Still, at the moment she really didn't know what else to do. If Jemini wanted her to buy the property then she would give it her best shot. Hopefully Jenna would be able to work miracles.

She checked in at the sheriff's department before starting her shift. Since patrol was not normally her detail and she was just filling in, she had a few cases of her own that needed attention. She stacked the folders in the center of her desk with plans to return later in the evening if the night was quiet.

She radioed dispatch that she was on duty and made a pass through Riverview, hitting every street before turning onto Rivers Pass. Brandon met her in the driveway, his face red and puffy. He wrapped his little arms around her waist and hugged her tight. Over his head, Steph could see Kim and Agnes on the front porch. Pulling Brandon with her, she walked toward them, her heart filled with dread.

"It's true then?" Kim asked.

Steph shook her head.

Kim stood and then sat again, clearly not sure what step to take next. "I just don't understand why Dorothy would do this to us."

They both looked at Agnes.

"Ms. Agnes?" Steph prodded her.

"She wanted her to come home," Agnes finally spoke.

"This is not her home." Steph didn't even try to keep the anger out of her voice.

Kim nodded. "I've never even met her and I've lived in Riverview for over ten years."

Agnes shrugged. "That's what Dorothy said. She wanted her to come home."

Steph sat down beside Brandon on the front steps. "She doesn't consider this her home. She told me she had no emotional ties to this place."

Kim's head whipped up. "You spoke with her. Oh, right, of course, you did. You were both at the reading of the will." She paused for a second. "What's she like? Can we change her mind?"

"That would be a good place to start," Agnes said softly.

Steph gave Agnes a hard glare. "She's the cold-hearted professional type, and I don't think we'll be able to change her mind. I applied for a loan, but she's asking a lot so don't get your hopes up."

Kim stood again. "Maybe if we all sign on the loan."

"That might work," Steph agreed. "I'll let you know when I hear from the bank."

Kim glanced at Agnes. "Are you in too?"

"Let's try to change her mind first."

Steph rolled her eyes. "She isn't that kind of person. We aren't going to be able to change her mind. We have to do something now."

"Please just try, Stephanie. For Dorothy." Agnes met her eyes and Steph saw all the years of Dorothy's pain mirrored there.

"Okay, Ms. Agnes." Steph stood. "I need to get back to work."

"Brandon, go get Ms. Steph's dinner. Quick." Kim urged him through the door to the stairs.

"You didn't have to do that, Kim, but I appreciate it."

Brandon flew back down the stairs and handed Steph a lunch bag. She gave him another hug. "We'll figure something out, buddy. Don't worry."

He gave her a halfhearted smile before returning to sit at his mom's feet.

Steph waved and climbed in her cruiser. Before pulling out on the main road, she unzipped the bag and pulled out the bottle of water. Checking the other contents, she found pasta salad and a baked chicken breast. She smiled at Kim's thoughtfulness as she looked at the chicken already cut into bite-sized pieces. It smelled good, but Steph wasn't sure she could keep down any food at the moment.

She pulled out onto the road and drove out of town to the farthest county limit. Her favorite part of working patrol was the solitary driving around. She liked to get away from people and think. Tonight, however, her thoughts were making her crazy. She couldn't analyze the situation with Jemini without making her head hurt. She considered stopping at Lake View, but at this time of the evening Cassie would be settled in with her family. She would never turn her away if she wanted to talk, but Steph wasn't sure she could handle Cassie's happiness on a night she felt so empty and lonely.

As she approached Rivers Pass again, she turned on a rutted side road where she could approach the house without Agnes noticing. She watched as the sun slowly set over Dorothy's house and thought about where she was supposed to go from here. She wasn't sure she could stay in her home if Agnes and Kim were evicted from theirs. Even if she helped them find new homes, she would be miserable there knowing she hadn't been able to stop it. She couldn't believe the burden Dorothy had put on her.

Thoughts of Dorothy brought thoughts of Jemini and how she wished she would have returned before Dorothy had died. She could imagine a different kind of meeting between them then. One where she didn't have to be angry and where she could explore the attraction she felt toward her. Finally forcing her focus back to work, she turned the cruiser around, heading back toward the main road.

After a suspicious activity call around ten p.m. that turned out to be two boys trying to catch worms for night fishing, Steph was finally able to return to the office and work on her case files. Currently she had two break-ins, one case of feuding neighbors, and a suspicious death which she was pretty sure would be ruled natural causes when the autopsy came back.

She typed up some interview notes but quickly realized most of what she needed to do couldn't be accomplished at one in the morning. Returning to her solitary driving, she let her mind ramble again through the events of the last week.

CHAPTER FIVE

Jemini stepped onto the porch, closing the door behind her. After a solitary dinner of saltine crackers and a glass of wine, she had slept a few hours. Unfortunately she felt as miserable today as she had yesterday. Dressed in the only pair of shorts she had brought and running shoes, she hoped a run would make her feel normal again. She would enjoy some fresh air and then drive back to Chattanooga.

"We seem to keep meeting like this." Kathleen smiled up at Jemini. "Would you like to walk?"

She stared longingly at the woods surrounding her but returned Kathleen's smile instead. The peace and serenity of the forest was calling her, but she also felt a strange pull to be around Kathleen. Her strength and confidence inspired a feeling of comfort. "Sure. Why not?"

"I was happy to see you return last night. Are you going to stay for the cookout tomorrow?"

"I'm sorry, but I don't think that would be a good idea."

Kathleen was silent for a few moments and then she asked, "Is it Steph?"

She gave Kathleen a quick glance. She wasn't the type to pour out her soul to an unknown stranger, but the compassion in Kathleen's face eased her resistance. Maybe getting some of it out would help her feel more settled. Kathleen was the perfect person too. Not just because she was easy to talk to but more so because Jemini planned to leave today and maybe never return.

"Dorothy Rivers was my grandmother. Apparently, Steph was close to her and she has been angry since I arrived, though I'm not sure why." She watched the sidewalk in front of them as she thought about Steph's question the night she arrived. "*Why are you here?*"

"Maybe she's upset because I didn't attend the funeral, but I didn't know she had passed away until two days ago when the attorney contacted me concerning the will."

"Maybe you'll get a chance to talk with Steph and explain that to her. I've only known her for a couple of months, but she seems pretty levelheaded."

After a few seconds of silence Kathleen spoke again. "Do you mind if I asked what happened at the reading of the will?"

"She left everything but Steph's house and ten acres to me."

"And that upsets you?"

"Yes." Jemini stopped walking. "I don't live here. The only thing I can do is sell it."

"You don't want to move here?"

"No!"

Kathleen placed her hand on Jemini's arm. "I'm sorry. I wasn't trying to upset you."

"It wasn't a very happy time for me when my mom took me away from here. I thought my grandmother was the world."

"Thought?"

"I eventually found out the truth."

"Oh."

Jemini shook her head. "I'm sorry. I guess you knew her too. It seems everyone in town did."

"Not really. I met her once, but I haven't lived in Riverview very long. We keep pretty busy here at the farm."

Jemini continued to study the path in front of them. She had shared with Kathleen and now she was going to ask Kathleen to do the same. She couldn't help being curious about how the town accepted them and their relationship. "Do you mind if I ask about you and Cassie?"

"Of course not. We met last summer and I couldn't make myself leave here."

"Because of Cassie or the farm?"

"Yes!"

Jemini laughed, happy to be discussing something other than her past. "So you and Cassie are together?"

"We are. Does that bother you?"

"Oh no. I'm a lesbian too. I just wondered about living in this small town."

"It's surprisingly open and believe it or not we aren't the only lesbians in town."

"I felt like a zoo animal at the diner yesterday. The town's really pretty diverse, all things considered. I thought maybe they hadn't seen a lesbian before."

Kathleen laughed. "No, I'm guessing that was because of your last name. Rivers is a big name around here and not just because of Dorothy. Your great-great-great-grandfather was the first official mayor of Riverview. Of course, it wasn't called Riverview back then. It was Landers Pass." Kathleen shrugged when Jemini gave her a puzzled look. "I was curious after you arrived the other night. Cassie couldn't tell me why the town of Riverview didn't have a river, so I went online and tried to find out. It does make more sense that the town was named after a person rather than a river that doesn't exist. Originally it was called Riversview, but somewhere along they dropped the 's' and it became Riverview."

"I didn't realize how far back my history went in this town. It wasn't something I cared about as a kid and after I became an adult it was too painful to even think about Riverview."

Jemini was silent while she thought about how she had been treated as a child by the people of Riverview. In the South, a child from a mixed-race family would usually face discrimination and harassment, but she could only remember feeling like royalty everywhere she went. Her mother had tried to teach her about racial inequality, but in Dorothy's shadow it wasn't something she had experienced. After they left, she had learned that race did influence how you were treated by others. Being an attorney had taught her to offer civility to others and expect it in return. Her expectations were normally met.

Jemini watched Kathleen's face as she switched the topic of conversation to get more answers. "Stephanie says there are tenants in the house. Do you know them?"

"Not really but Cassie does. Apparently, Ms. Agnes has lived in this town her whole life. She used to own a beauty shop in Riverview. I think she's in her seventies now so she's been retired for a number of years. Kim and her ten-year-old son Brandon live upstairs. Chase and Brandon are in the same class at school."

"The attorney never mentioned anything like that when he called about the reading of the will. I asked not to be present, but he said I needed to be because of what was being left to me. He implied it was the house and I made it clear I had no intention of moving here no matter what was left to me. He'd already set things up with a realtor, but I didn't realize there was still someone living there."

"Of course you didn't. Why would you?"

"Maybe I'll be able to sell it to someone that will let them stay."

As they neared the office on their second lap, Kathleen paused. "I guess I should go back to work. So, you're staying another day then?"

"I'm not sure. Maybe."

"Okay. Well, I hope so. I'm enjoying our morning walks."

She smiled as she started up the hill toward the wooded path. She needed to call Karen and see what time she was supposed to be in front of Judge Stevens tomorrow afternoon, but she couldn't remember the last time she didn't have anywhere she needed to be immediately. She didn't have to be in any hurry to leave this quiet paradise. As she entered the shaded canopy, she allowed herself to consider the things she was growing to like in Riverview.

She could start with the town's very attractive deputy sheriff and the unknown pull she felt whenever she was near her, but she didn't want to think about Stephanie and the emotional roller-coaster ride she was on with her. It was hard, however, not to think about the good things she had seen in her in the last two days. Stephanie clearly had a personal connection with the tenants in Dorothy's house and even though she had been given security in what Dorothy had left her, she was still worried about them.

She did want to know why Stephanie was so mad at her, though. If it was because she didn't come to the funeral then she hoped she would have a chance to explain. If it was because she had left Riverview, it was hard to believe Stephanie had held onto her anger for twenty years. She had been sad when they left, but she had never once felt anger toward Stephanie. She knew she had been rude yesterday when they talked, but she couldn't believe that Stephanie thought for one minute that she would throw away her current life and rush to live in Riverview. She couldn't help but hope that Stephanie would allow her a chance to explain that as well.

Comfortable with her pace, Jemini settled into the rhythm of her run. With her busy schedule she couldn't remember the last time she had been able to go for a run and not be on a time restraint or to enjoy the outdoors. Her workouts usually consisted of a treadmill inside an air-conditioned gym.

As her stress began to fade, she knew she couldn't leave Riverview without talking to Stephanie. They had issues to work out between them. She had thought she could sever the ties again and return to her life, but the truth was she felt connected to Stephanie somehow. She wanted the chance for them to talk civilly. There was a chance that Stephanie held the answers to questions she didn't even know she wanted to ask.

* * *

Steph couldn't stop her truck from turning in at Lake View. She had thought all evening about Agnes's words and how she might convince Jemini to stay in Riverview. She parked in front of the office and looked around. She loved this place. It was almost like another world where things were quieter and moved at a slower pace. She turned at the sound of horse hooves thundering across the pasture and spotted Cassie and Chase riding hard. She started walking toward the barn to meet them. She was relieved to hear their laughter and see two happy faces as they dismounted.

"The way you guys were riding I thought there was a bear chasing you."

"No bear, Ms. Steph. Just trying to win ice cream for dessert," Chase said excitedly.

Cassie laughed. "You win, Chase. Now you get to cool down both horses while I talk to Ms. Steph."

"It's worth it!" Chase said as he unstrapped his saddle and pulled it from the horse. It looked as big as he was, but he handled it with expertise, lugging it over to the saddle stand and swinging it up into place.

"He's a hard worker especially if there's ice cream or horses involved." Cassie smiled at Steph. "What's going on with you?"

"Just looking for someone to help me straighten out my head."

Cassie threw her arm around Steph's shoulders. "You've come to the right place. Let's get some coffee."

Steph smiled as Kathleen looked up when they entered the office. Her eyes narrowed. "What are you two up to?"

"Steph came for some advice."

"Then I'll leave you two alone."

"No, Kathleen. Can you stay?" Steph asked. "You still kinda have an outsider's point of view. That can be useful."

Steph took the chair by the window, staring back and forth between them. Kathleen's eyes never left Cassie as she brewed each cup of coffee in the Keurig. She had given up on finding someone to share her life with a long time ago. Getting close and then the pain of leaving was more than she thought she could stand. Watching Cassie and Kathleen made her believe in love again, if only a little bit.

She knew their lives had been complicated in the beginning, but she would never forget the night Cassie had called her to issue an Amber Alert because Chase was missing. She had seen a change in Cassie that night and even the next morning when they found Chase safe, but very scared. During the police interviews she had conducted later to find out exactly what Chase had seen the night his foster parent was murdered, Cassie and Kathleen had barely left his side. Neither of them was his birth mother, but there wasn't any doubt that they both had developed a mother-and-child relationship with him. During that time, she had also gotten to know Kathleen, who worked with a foster care organization in Pensacola that placed kids on rural farms for the summer. Her impact on Cassie had gone far beyond what could be seen by the human eye. They completed each other as well as making each a better person. She had to admit she had stayed longer than the interviews with Chase had warranted in order to be around the warmth of their family.

"Okay, Steph, let's hear it." Cassie handed her a cup of coffee, pulling her away from her thoughts.

She took a deep breath and went straight to the heart of the situation. She was here to ask their advice so no need to sugarcoat the topic. "Agnes says Dorothy wanted Jemini to come home and that it's up to us to convince her to stay."

"And did Dorothy leave any suggestions on how to do that?" Cassie asked, handing Kathleen a cup too.

"No, and I can't seem to talk with Jemini for more than two seconds without getting angry. I want to be furious with Dorothy, but I can't make myself because I miss her so much." She choked back a sob. She thought she had handled Dorothy's funeral and all the ensuing memorial dinners well. She had remained strong, helping Agnes get from place to place, but she hadn't really taken time to allow herself to mourn, she now realized. When all this was over she would take some time to cry, she decided, even though she wasn't really the crying type. Given all this stuff with Jemini, though, she was afraid she wasn't going to have control of the emotions when they finally decided to take over.

"Oh, Steph." Cassie took the seat opposite her and leaned forward, her elbows resting on her knees. "I don't think Dorothy meant to make things rougher on you. She saw an opportunity to bring her granddaughter home."

Kathleen's voice was low as if to soften the blow of her words. "It'll be hard to convince Jemini to walk away from her job. She has a life in Tennessee."

"I know," Steph sighed, pushing the tears back. "But I have to try." Kathleen's words held the truth even if she didn't want to hear them. "Do you think telling her how much Dorothy wanted her to come home would help or make things worse?"

"That's a tough question," Cassie answered, glancing at Kathleen.

"I think it would help," Kathleen said. "Right now, she doesn't understand where you're coming from. Just talking is good, though. Especially if you can tell her why you're so angry."

Steph nodded. She had suspected, but now she knew for sure. Kathleen's words were more than her opinion. Jemini had been talking to her. She was glad she had asked Kathleen to remain for the conversation. "Do you guys know if she's in her cabin right now?"

Kathleen pointed out the window and Steph's gaze instantly found the outline of a familiar figure walking down the hill toward the resort. Even from a distance, she could see every curve of Jemini's body highlighted by the yellow shirt and black shorts. She didn't need Cassie or Kathleen to encourage her. "I'm going to talk to her," she said as she hurried out the door.

She stood on the steps to Jemini's cabin and waited for her to approach. Jemini's beautiful brown thighs were toned and the muscles in them tightened with each step she took. As hard as she tried, she couldn't pull her eyes away from the body in front of her. The yellow running shirt hugged Jemini's chest, revealing breasts that the suit had hidden yesterday. She looked different and not just because of the clothes she was wearing. Her expression seemed softer somehow and more inviting.

* * *

"What can I do for you, Deputy Williams?"
"I thought we could try to talk again."

"I'm listening." Jemini motioned to the chairs on the porch of her cabin. She would hear what Stephanie had to say and maybe ask some questions of her own, but she didn't want to talk about what she was going to do with her inheritance. The last thing she wanted was for Stephanie to realize she had a sliver of doubt about selling Dorothy's house.

"I thought you should know that Dorothy left you the house in hopes you would return to Riverview."

Jemini nodded. She had already come to that conclusion, but the truth was Dorothy didn't know the person Jemini had become. "She wouldn't have done that if she'd known me."

Stephanie frowned. "What does that mean?"

"It means just what I said. Dorothy didn't know me."

She could see the confusion on Stephanie's face, but she wasn't ready to say the words out loud. Telling anyone that her grandmother wouldn't love her because of the way she chose to live her life wasn't an easy statement.

"How can I convince you Riverview is great place to live?"

"That's really not open to discussion. My life is in Tennessee. I'm not going to move here." Jemini knew her answer was brusque, but she was getting sick of everyone just assuming she would drop her life and move to Riverview.

The glimpse of rage that flashed across Stephanie's face made her take a step back. She didn't know why she couldn't have a normal conversation with her. Every time they met they engaged in a duel of words that neither of them seemed to win. Stephanie's face was still flushed as she stepped off the porch and raised her arms in defeat.

"I guess I'm wasting my time then."

She could hear the sadness in Stephanie's voice and she remembered all the questions she wanted to ask. "What do you want from me, Stephanie?"

"I want my friend back."

She watched Stephanie's back as she climbed in her truck and roared away. It annoyed her to feel confused and intrigued at the same time.

"I want my friend back."

Well, she couldn't bring Dorothy back. No matter what she did with the house it wouldn't change the fact that Dorothy had died, leaving them all in this precarious position. Stephanie was going to have to grow up and stop living in the past. She wasn't going to feel sorry for her. Stephanie had gotten to live the life that should have been hers. She was the one who should have been raised by a grandmother who cared about her instead of living with haunting memories of a love that stopped in a second because of someone's actions or beliefs. She had never seen it, but she knew love wasn't supposed to be attached to things. It was supposed to be unconditional. Dorothy's love hadn't been.

She slammed the door behind her as she entered the cabin. So much for getting Stephanie to answer her questions. She'd have to live without them. She pulled her cell phone from her pocket and dialed her office. Pressing it to her ear, she set her computer on the counter in front of her and opened her email. After listening to Karen's sugary greeting, Jemini interrupted her.

"Hey, Karen. Do you have the details for tomorrow yet?"

"Yes, the judge will meet you in his chambers at one."

"In his chambers? Not in the courtroom?"

"Apparently they're bringing the kids too."

"Did something happen?"

"Not that I'm aware of."

"Okay. I'll call around and see if I can find something out."

"Let me know if you need anything from me. When are you coming back?"

She sighed. When was she going home? She had been adamant that Riverview wasn't her home and that she wouldn't stay longer than she needed to. Now she seemed to be having trouble pulling herself away from a place she hadn't wanted to come to in the first place. "I'll swing by the office about noon before I head over to the courthouse."

"You're still in the boonies?"

"I am, but I'm trying to wrap things up." *Am I really?*

"Okay. See you tomorrow."

She disconnected from Karen and dialed a friend in the dispatcher's office. All emergency calls went through there. Darren would know if something criminal or medical had happened. While she waited for him to answer, she tried to think what she should do before leaving Riverview tomorrow. She realized she wanted to go to Dorothy's house. She wanted to reminisce one last time before she erased Dorothy from her mind forever.

Besides, Mr. Cross had said they would throw everything out when the house sold and that felt wrong to her. Someone who cared about Dorothy should go through her stuff and sort it. Jemini was a little bit surprised that Stephanie hadn't asked to do so. Maybe she already had. It seemed reasonable that Stephanie or Dorothy's tenants would have a key to her place too. She would stop by and talk with them. Even if they didn't want to sort anything, they should have the opportunity to take a keepsake. The truth was she wanted to meet them. She wanted to put faces with names. Maybe she would find Stephanie too and they could try again to talk about why she was so angry.

"Hey, Darren. Were the police or EMS dispatched to the Watson house again?" she asked when she was routed to his desk.

"Jemini. It's good to talk with you, too. I've been fine. Thanks for asking."

"Sorry. I'm in a hurry."

"You're always in a hurry. Let me check the logs."

She listened as his fingers flitted across the keys. Darren was one of the few people in her life she could count on. Granted he didn't provide anything more than work-related information, but he always came through for her.

"I don't see anything. No, wait. Not dispatched for what you'd think. The kids showed up at their parents' house and Mrs. Watson called the police to pick them up."

"Crap. I guess they ran from the state home back to their parents. I was afraid that would happen what with the judge taking so long to hear their case."

"It looks like after some tears they returned willingly. Good thing Mrs. Watson called. Keeping them would have really hurt her case."

"Yep. Thanks, Darren."

"Call me sometime when you're not in a hurry and only want to use me for information."

Jemini smiled as she pressed the disconnect button. She was pretty sure Darren was gay, but just in case he wasn't she was careful not to encourage him. Thinking of not encouraging someone made her think of Robin. Glancing at her watch, she dialed Robin's cell. Hopefully she could catch her between hospital shifts.

"Jemini. Are you back in town?" Robin asked without a greeting.

Surprisingly, Robin sounded happy to hear from her. She wondered if she was about to make a mistake. Robin never put any relationship pressure on her. She was free to come and go and to work as much as she wanted. Past girlfriends usually were sick of her schedule after the first week—one of the many reasons she didn't stay with anyone very long. Work always came first even if someone was holding dinner at home for her. She couldn't remember ever wanting to drop anything and hurry home. In fact, she wasn't really sure she knew where home was.

She took a deep breath before telling Robin the truth. She couldn't help but wonder if this would be the time she objected to her schedule. "No. It's taking longer than I expected here."

"I was off yesterday and had nothing to do."

She should have known Robin's self-interest would be the only response she received. She hated being made to feel guilty. "I'm sure you figured something out."

"Well, yeah. Mary and some friends came by, so I went out with them."

Jemini was reminded again how incompatible she and Robin were. Their busy schedules was the draw in the beginning. She had been sick of being hounded for never coming home, and when she met Robin, an emergency room nurse, who worked sixteen-hour shifts five or six days a week, it had seemed like an ideal match. She had discovered quickly that Robin liked to party on her days off, but at the time having an occasional girlfriend for company had seemed okay.

"So why did you call if you're not back in town?" she heard Robin ask.

I'm not sure. "It might be a while longer before I can return." She wasn't sure why she didn't mention that she would be returning the next day for court. She could have stayed at her condo with Robin, but was thinking instead about returning in time for the cookout. Which meant that she actually did know why she didn't mention it. She didn't want to make time to see Robin. She would go and do what she had to do and then return to Riverview.

"Okay. Well, call me when you get back into town."

She listened to the empty line before clicking her phone off. Robin wasn't girlfriend material; she needed to end things between them. Breaking up over the phone was not her style, but she dialed Robin's number again anyway.

"What now?"

"Why are you being so short with me?" she asked, irritated that Robin's attitude made her feel defensive and wondering if Robin could sense her real reason for calling.

"I didn't get much sleep last night, and if I can finish here quickly I might catch a nap before the night gets crazy."

"Okay. I'm sorry. I just wanted to clear things up between us in case I don't come back for a while."

Robin was silent for a minute and she hoped she was interpreting her meaning.

"That's fine," Robin finally said.

"Okay, good."

"Good night."

She found herself listening to the dial tone again.

After a quick shower, she climbed in her car and went in search of food. She didn't think she could stand another meal at the diner with everyone watching her so she settled instead for a soggy convenience store tuna fish sandwich and chips. Sitting in her car while she ate, she watched the grass-covered commons in the center of town. It was fairly busy this sunny afternoon and she was fascinated to note that everyone stopped to talk to each other. She wondered if she walked across the circle if anyone would stop to talk with her.

Around the circle was a scattering of 1800s and 1900s buildings. A large red brick building stretched the length of one side with a simple explanation of its purpose written across the white trim over the white pillars: "Restaurant, Bar, Lodging." Simple yet elegant. The next building was slightly more modern with white siding and huge glass windows. Berkeley County Bank was engraved at the top. Underneath that was a smaller sign announcing which chain bank currently held possession. Other small businesses dotted the circle, including a beauty shop, a pet store, the lawyer's office, the real estate office, and an electronics store. Of course, somewhere nearby would be a hardware store. Something small that the locals used. A larger chain one would be outside of town near the Walmart.

She liked that Riverview had maintained its quaint status. Over the years, the town had refused to give up its historic personality. Remembering Kathleen's history tale from that morning, she wondered about her grandfathers. She had stopped thinking about her past being attached to Dorothy's a long time ago, but now that she knew her family had helped to make this town what it was today she felt a sense of pride as she looked around. This was her town. She could stay and make a home here. If Cassie and Kathleen were any indication, then a lesbian wouldn't be run out of town, and with Dorothy gone there was no one left for her to disgrace.

She tossed her trash into a can on the street and entered the lawyer's office. The same receptionist sat at the desk.

"Is Mr. Cross in?"

"He's in a meeting right now. Can I relay a message for you?"

"I would like to have the keys to Dorothy, uh, Ms. Rivers' house?"

"Sure. Just a minute."

She paced the small carpeted room while she waited. She wasn't sure what she planned to do and she wasn't sure she was happy with herself for doing it. Standing outside with the sun shining on her, she had allowed herself to consider making this town her home. Now reality was sinking in and that idea seemed crazy. Rather than walk out now, though, and look even crazier, she would wait for the receptionist to return. Seeing the inside of Dorothy's house and meeting the tenants was still on her list of things to do. The receptionist returned a few minutes later and handed her a ring with several keys attached.

"He said to remind you about the tenants if you're going out to the house."

She nodded. How could she forget about the people that she could end up evicting from their homes? If she did nothing else in this town, she would make sure that those people weren't made homeless.

CHAPTER SIX

Jemini retrieved the bags from her second stop at the convenience store from the seat beside her and slid from the car. She needed comfort food, and the store had provided chips, candy, chocolate, and several bottles of Dr. Pepper. Remembering the curtain moving on the right side and assuming that one was occupied, she juggled the bags as she unlocked the door on the left side of the porch. As the door opened, she was instantly bombarded by memories of the past. Even after twenty years, Dorothy's living room appeared the same, including the rocking chair where they had rocked together. The smell of cookies baking was so strong she went into the kitchen to make sure there weren't any in the oven. She dropped her bags on the kitchen table, pulling open a plastic container of Gummy Worms. Grabbing three floppy fruit-flavored gummies, she began walking through the house.

There were a few changes but nothing big. She allowed herself to remember her childhood memories. Feelings of comfort and warmth flooded through her and she saw the house through the eyes of a child. Dorothy's laughter flowed as she reminded Jemini to wipe her feet at the door before bringing her latest find into the house. A pine cone, a rock that looked like something cool, or maybe even an insect. Nothing was turned away from Dorothy's examination. If it was living, she was told to return it to where she found it, but the non-living items always found a place of honor within the house.

A knock on the door startled her and she pulled the door open without looking. Stephanie stood on the porch, grinning. Jemini waved the remaining Gummy Worms at her. "If you're just here to fight with me, don't bother. I've had enough for today."

Stephanie dropped her head, giving her a contrite look. "I'm sorry. I do seem to have difficulty controlling my temper around you."

"Want to tell me why?"

"No, counselor. I'm not here to visit our past. I'm here to invite you to dinner."

Jemini took a bite of her Gummy Worm and chewed slowly. "And why would I want to dine with you?"

"Well, it's not with me. It's with Ms. Agnes next door. I have to work."

"Why didn't she come invite me herself?"

"I think she might be afraid of you."

Jemini frowned, but it quickly faded as she followed Stephanie's gaze to the Gummy Worms in her hand. Violently, she bit another one in half and swallowed it. "As she should be."

Stephanie laughed. "You're still a little crazy, aren't you? So what should I tell Ms. Agnes?"

She dropped into a nearby chair. "I don't know." She had been enjoying the banter with Stephanie, but now the seriousness of the situation once again was sinking in on her. She had wanted to meet the tenants, but now that idea didn't seem so good. What had Dorothy told them about her? Or about her mother?

Stephanie stepped in front of her and reached out her hand. "Come meet her and if you aren't sure, you can bow out gracefully."

She stared at Stephanie's outstretched hand and slowly reached her hand up to meet it. Stephanie wrapped their fingers together and warmth spread through her. She caught her breath and pushed aside any romantic feelings. Stephanie wasn't a lesbian. She couldn't be. She had spent her life with Dorothy, so that couldn't have happened.

Touching a straight woman shouldn't bring this reaction, she warned herself. She knew she should pull away, but she didn't want to. She stood and let Stephanie lead her through the living room into a large shared foyer.

* * *

Steph knocked on the door directly across the foyer, giving Jemini's hand a squeeze. She wasn't sure why she had offered her hand to her except that she had looked so vulnerable when presented with the idea of facing Agnes, a tenant in the house she was trying to sell.

"Is this my stalker?" Agnes asked as she pulled open the door.

Steph laughed but stopped suddenly after she glanced at Jemini. Jemini's face looked shocked and her breathing had slowed. Guiding Jemini to a chair in the foyer, she pushed her onto it. She knelt beside her, still holding tight to her hand.

"I remember you," Jemini said, her voice barely more than a whisper. "You gave us candy."

Steph laughed. "Every time she cut our hair, we could pick a piece of candy from the bowl on the counter. Everyone thought I liked short hair, but really I was after the candy."

Jemini smiled weakly and rubbed her face before glancing at Agnes again. Agnes still stood in the doorway holding the door open. Steph wasn't sure if they were going to be asked to leave and she frowned at Agnes.

"So, this is my stalker?" Agnes repeated.

Steph looked at the confusion on Jemini's face and explained. "You came by the house yesterday but didn't get out of the car?"

"Oh, yes." Jemini's dark skin developed a pink hue as she realized what Agnes meant. "I'm sorry. I wanted to see the house. To see if it still looked the same."

"And does it?" Agnes demanded.

Over Jemini's shoulder, Steph glared at Agnes again. It was Agnes's idea to convince Jemini to stay in Riverview and now she was being so unfriendly Steph wasn't sure she even wanted to stay in the room with her.

"Yes," Jemini answered. "It does look the same."

"So, why did you come back to Riverview?"

"I came for the reading of the will."

"To see what Dorothy had left for you?" Agnes continued her barrage.

"Agnes," Steph said, hoping her tone would caution Agnes on her harshness.

Jemini ignored their interaction. Her eyes focused on Agnes. "No. No, I don't want anything from her."

"And yet you're here taking what she left."

"I'm not keeping it." Jemini seemed shocked by Agnes's words.

"I want to sit outside," Agnes announced.

Jemini stood. "I should go. I'm sorry, but I won't be able to make it to dinner. Thank you for the offer."

Steph looked back and forth between them. Her hopes that Agnes would charm Jemini into staying were destroyed. In all her years, she had never seen Agnes act like she just had. She watched Jemini step back into the other half of the house before she exploded on Agnes.

"What the hell!"

"I was shaking her up. Making her think."

"You made her think all right. She's thinking now that she won't stay a minute longer than she has to."

Agnes smiled. "I want to sit on the porch. Sit with me."

Since it was more a statement than a question, she followed. She was so confused by Agnes's actions. They had all talked about how Jemini needed to be convinced to stay or at least not to sell the house and Agnes had been almost cruel with her. "I don't understand you."

"She's too caught up in her world. She needs to remember. Help her remember."

Steph dropped onto the porch steps as memories of her childhood flooded in. She and Jemini sitting in this spot eating homemade ice cream cones. Her dad in his wide-brimmed hat, riding the mower across the yard. Her mom and Dorothy on the porch, listening patiently to each wild tale Jemini could make up. Steph had never been good at lying and she still wasn't. Being a cop came naturally to her. Everything was either black or white; there was no gray in her world.

She stood. "I'm going to talk to Jemini."

"Good idea." Agnes's chair rocked back and forth.

* * *

Jemini pushed the door closed and collapsed against it. She wasn't sure what she had expected from the seventy-year-old woman next door, but she was sure she hadn't gotten it. What she had gotten instead was a slap in the face. Why was she stressing over selling the house? She should just sell it and get out of this town forever.

She pulled a bag of dark chocolate caramels from the counter and unwrapped one. Washing it down with Dr. Pepper, she opened the bag of Cherry Sours. She tossed several in her mouth as she walked around the room, looking at the pictures on the wall and on the mantel. She stopped in front of the last picture on the mantel and stared into her father's face, trying to see a piece of herself within him. He looked happy enough as he leaned against his Ford convertible, holding little Jemini in his arms, his red, sunburned face pressed tightly against her curly black hair. There were pictures of her and her mother too, but she couldn't find any with the three of them together.

She didn't think about her father much. In truth, Dorothy's only son hadn't been much of a father. He was a truck driver, against his mother's wishes, and on the road a lot more than he was home. She couldn't remember spending a Christmas with him or receiving any presents from him. She could remember Dorothy's tears at his funeral, though. She had been too young to grieve for something she hadn't really had. Her father hadn't been home and now he wasn't ever coming home—it seemed like the same thing to her at age thirteen.

Living with Grandma Dorothy was all she had ever known. She didn't know why Dorothy had invited Jake and his new wife to live with her. Maybe because Jake was gone so much and Aries was so young. Or maybe simply because she wanted to. Aries's parents had been elderly when they adopted her as a baby and had passed away before her marriage to Jake. Aries had grown up moving from hippie camp to hippie camp and was eager to call a single place home. Whatever the reason, Dorothy's house became the only true home Aries and Jemini ever knew.

Staring into her father's eyes, Jemini remembered that he had given her something after all. Not only his last name but the J from his first name as well. Aries's parents' final statement in rebelling against societal norms and anything conventional had been to name their child after the first sign in the Zodiac. In remembrance of them, Aries insisted her child carry a Zodiac name as well. She and Jake had compromised by changing Gemini to Jemini.

Even now the thought of her father's passing didn't evoke any painful feelings for her. Being ripped from the house after thirteen years had been much more painful. It was time to close that chapter, move on. She popped a few more Cherry Sours into her mouth. She felt at peace with her decision to sell the house now. Despite the hostility that she'd just received from Agnes, she would, however, try to make sure whoever bought it was willing to keep the tenants.

With that weight lifted off her shoulders, she found herself curious about the life she had left so long ago. She didn't want to snoop through Dorothy's personal stuff—she would leave that for Stephanie or Agnes. But maybe she could find some pictures of her childhood to take with her. She pulled open a closet door beside the bathroom, expecting to find sheets or towels, but instead found coats and shoes with a few shoe boxes across the top. She pulled down the first one and found a pair of shoes that appeared to never have been worn. The second box was harder to reach, but it contained shoes too. The third box balanced on the small shelf, and she stretched, pulling it slowly toward her. It wasn't as heavy as the others and it slid easily, gaining momentum as she stumbled backward, bracing for an inevitable fall.

"Jemini, what are you…?"

Jemini felt strong arms wrap around her waist. She leaned into Stephanie, allowing her to steady her movement with the box above her head. Her heart raced at the contact of their bodies and she dropped the box on a nearby chair. She waited a brief second for Stephanie to step back and when she didn't Jemini boldly turned in her arms.

A fluttering erupted in her stomach at the look of desire on Stephanie's face. Their lips inches apart, Jemini leaned slowly against her, sliding her hands up Stephanie's arms. Grasping the tie that held Stephanie's hair, Jemini released it and ran her fingers through the strands. With a slight touch on the back of Stephanie's head, she closed the distance between them, her body humming with pleasure as their lips met. She moaned, opening her mouth to Stephanie's tongue and deepening the kiss.

She gave no thought to the fact that she was kissing a straight woman or what the consequences of that might be. The way they were kissing didn't feel wrong. Jemini's head screamed for her to stop, but her body resisted the command. As if Stephanie could hear the internal exchange, she stepped back and broke off the kiss. They each stared at the other until finally Stephanie broke the silence.

"What the hell are you eating?"

Jemini frowned and then began laughing as she crossed to the kitchen counter, holding up the bag of Cherry Sours candy.

Stephanie took the bag from her and wrinkled her nose. "These are disgusting. Balls of cherry-flavored sugar."

"You seemed to like them a moment ago."

"No, I liked you until I tasted your tongue."

Her heart stopped again. Stephanie liked tasting her. Could she be wrong? Was the attraction she felt for her possibly real? Stephanie couldn't be a lesbian, could she? Pushing the contradicting thoughts from her mind, she laughed again and waved a Gummy Worm at her. "Want to get rid of the taste?"

"What are you doing here? Having a junk food festival? The only thing missing is a Twinkie."

"Make that deep fried and I'll take it."

"Oh, man." Stephanie ran her fingers through her hair, pushing it back out of her eyes. "I saw you running this morning and I thought you cared about your health. You're killing your body."

"Are we avoiding talking about what just happened?"

"I'm not avoiding anything but a sugar coma. You, on the other hand, are lucky to be alive."

She placed her hand on Stephanie's arm to stop the banter. "What just happened between us?"

Stephanie dropped the bag of Cherry Sours on the counter and took a step back. Watching her retreat brought back all Jemini's doubts from moments ago. Maybe Stephanie really wasn't a lesbian and didn't feel what she had.

Her eyes still locked with Jemini's, Stephanie shrugged. "I'm not sure. Are you still selling the house?"

"It keeps coming back to this."

"I'm afraid so. I don't fool around for fun. I'm looking for something more permanent."

Stephanie was out the door before Jemini could respond. She was too stunned to speak. *What did she mean by that? Something "more permanent?" With her?*

She couldn't believe that Stephanie had walked out in the middle of a conversation again, but the truth was she was partially relieved. She wanted something more permanent too, she realized, and in a few more seconds she might have uttered those words out loud. In front of Stephanie. She leaned against the counter and stared at the bag of Cherry Sours candy. She did want something more permanent. Just not in Riverview. Or with a straight woman.

A knock on the door brought her back from her thoughts. *Stephanie?* She hoped it was, but what if it was Agnes? She crossed to the window and pulled back the curtain. Richard Greene stood on the porch with his briefcase in his hands. She opened the door but didn't invite him in.

"Hello, Richard."

"Ms. Rivers, I have some really good news. I found a buyer. I have all the paperwork for you to sign right here. You'll have to return the day of the closing, but otherwise you're finished here and can head home."

She was stunned. It was what she had thought she had wanted, but that was before she heard about the tenants.

"Will they let the tenants remain?"

"Well," he said, avoiding her eyes. "Probably not. I believe they plan to develop the property. It would be really good for Riverview. New houses, stores, and restaurants."

Jemini felt sick. He didn't say the words tear down the house, but she heard them anyway. "What about Stephanie's house? That property belongs to her."

"The developer will make her a really good offer too. I can't imagine she'll be able to say no. Everything's going to be great."

She thought about Kim and Brandon, who she hadn't met yet, and wondered if they would feel the same way. Or Agnes. Even after their tense meeting earlier, she couldn't let this happen.

"I'm not sure about this, Richard. Let me think about it, okay?"

"Okay, but don't wait too long. This developer is looking at a lot of different properties and we don't want to miss out on his offer."

As she watched the real estate agent climb into his car, she was relieved to see that Agnes was no longer sitting on the porch. Richard's news made her nauseous, but having Agnes hear what he said wouldn't have been good. She crossed to the steps and sat down. Why didn't she just tell Richard no? She knew she couldn't sell to someone who was planning to tear down the house. She couldn't even consider an offer like that.

"Hello."

She looked up to see a small, black-haired little boy in cargo shorts and a tank top standing in front of her. The dark olive color of his face was richer than the sun would have produced this early in the year but lighter than her own skin color. His thick black eyebrows shaded his dark eyes, but she could see a ready smile waiting hesitantly on his round face. His knees were dirty, and there were muddy streaks on the cargo shorts where he had wiped his hands.

"Hello." She smiled at him.

"Are you Ms. Jemini?"

"I am. Are you Brandon?"

"Yes." He flopped onto the steps beside her.

"Mom says you're not coming to dinner. You don't like us?"

Surprised at his honesty, she searched for the words a little boy would understand. "I like you just fine. I'm not sure Ms. Agnes would be too happy with me being there."

"Yeah, we heard. Ms. Steph said she was rude. I'm not sure what that means, but Mom tells me I'm rude when I burp out loud. Did Ms. Agnes do that when you met her?"

She held in her laughter but couldn't stop a smile from spreading across her face. "No, she didn't do that."

"Oh."

"She just wasn't very friendly when I met her earlier."

Brandon wrinkled his face in thought. "I think maybe she's scared."

"Scared?"

"Well, she's old and all. I think she's scared you'll make her go away. I'm not scared. Mom says I'm young and I can go anywhere."

She thought about Brandon's words. Maybe Agnes was scared. She wished she could tell them all that everything would be okay, but she wasn't sure she could make that promise. What if the developer's was the only offer she received? Would she have to go with it? How long was she willing to wait? She wasn't sure, but she knew it would be wrong to say something she wasn't completely sure of. She would do her best, but eventually she would have to take whatever she was offered. "You might be right, Brandon. You're pretty smart."

"Mom says it's because I'm an only child."

"Will you ask your mom if I can come for dinner another day?"

Brandon jumped to his feet with a huge smile on his face and she heard him call as he disappeared. "She'll say yes."

She wasn't sure if he was coming back or not, but she'd had all she could take for one day. The emotional ups and downs of meeting Agnes and the haunting memory of Stephanie's kiss wouldn't go away easy. She locked Dorothy's front door and climbed into her car, glancing over at Stephanie's house. She could walk over there now and demand that she explain her actions, but she couldn't blame everything that happened on Stephanie. She had wanted to feel Stephanie's arms around her. Wanted to feel the softness of her lips. And at this moment, hearing the truth didn't sound like it would be very enjoyable. Stephanie wasn't a lesbian. She couldn't be.

It wasn't fair. She had finally found a woman who stirred her interest and it wasn't a woman she could have.

CHAPTER SEVEN

Steph had seen Richard leaving. The spring in his step made her uneasy, but she didn't believe Jemini would sell them out so quickly. She didn't want to anyway. She knew she should have stayed and talked things out with her. Kissing her without an invitation was probably not the best way to convince her to stay in Riverview, but she had lost all ability to think when Jemini had turned in her arms. She was still reeling from the kiss. Jemini was a captivating woman; the more she was around her the more she wanted. She tried to think about work as she put on her uniform, but it was everything she could do not to find Jemini and continue what they had started.

She wasn't surprised that Jemini's car was gone when she left for work. After the way Agnes had treated her and then the kiss, Jemini was probably scrambling to get out of town. She resisted the urge to drive to Lake View and see if she was still there. She wondered what Dorothy would think of her feelings for Jemini. She didn't have to wonder really. She could hear Dorothy's voice telling her she was crazy, that she had known

Jemini for only two days and it had taken just one kiss to knock her off her feet.

Dispatch radioed that they had a landline call for her and she accepted. They patched the call through to her cell phone.

"Deputy Williams?"

"Yes, ma'am. How can I help you?"

"I filed a report with you a couple of weeks ago about my garage being broken in to. You said to call if I noticed anything out of the ordinary."

"I remember. You live on Wymer Street, right?"

"Yes. When I came home from work tonight, I noticed footprints around my house. Right up at the windows. Like someone was looking in."

Steph didn't like what that implied, but she kept her tone neutral. "Is it okay if I come over now and look around before it gets dark?"

"That would be great."

She could hear relief in the woman's voice.

"Just stay inside until I get there, okay?"

"Yes, yes."

She disconnected the call and flipped on the cruiser's emergency lights. She didn't think the woman was in any real danger at the moment, but after dark her prowler might return. She couldn't afford to lose any daylight and Wymer Street was on the other side of town. Traffic was thin on a Thursday night and she only had to tap her siren twice to get the few cars out of her way.

She pulled the file up on her computer as soon as she stopped in front of the house on Wymer and quickly reviewed the circumstances surrounding the break-in. Sondra Pace did not have a deadbeat boyfriend or even an ex-boyfriend. She worked at one of the city offices and didn't appear to hang with the wrong crowd. There were nine other houses on this block and she had spoken to each of the other homeowners. No one else had had any break-ins or thefts that they were aware of at the time of the interview.

She exited her car and crossed to Sondra's porch, tapping lightly on the door. The curtain to the side of the door moved briefly before the door opened. Sondra Pace was a bit shorter than Steph with hair so blond it was almost white. She wore a heavy terry cloth robe over gray sweatpants and slippers on her feet.

"Hello, Ms. Pace. I'm going to be out here walking around your house and I didn't want to scare you."

"Okay. The footprints are all around the house behind the bushes. I wasn't going to bother you, but the longer I thought about it the more nervous they made me. It really looks like they were looking in the windows."

"I'm glad you called. Close all your blinds and make sure your windows are locked before it gets dark. I'll let you know before I leave."

Sondra nodded and stepped back inside.

Circling the house, Steph leaned between the bushes to study the footprints in the dirt. She tried to remember the last time it had rained. There wasn't any reason someone should be this close to the house and she made a mental note to ask about a pest control service.

When she finished, she knocked on Sondra's door again. "All windows locked and secured?"

"The one in the spare room won't close enough to lock, but the screen is in place."

"Do you mind if I look at it?"

"No. It's this way."

She followed Sondra down the narrow hallway into the first room facing the rear of the house. If she was trying to break in, this would definitely be the room she would choose. It was one of the few windows not in view of any of the neighbors or the street.

"Do you have a board or a piece of wood? I can wedge it so the window can't be opened."

"I might in the garage." She followed Sondra back through the house and into the garage, flipping on the light as they entered.

"My father liked to build stuff in here, and I haven't had a chance to clear all his stuff out yet. Feel free to look around."

Steph sorted through several pieces of wood that had been tossed under the workbench until she found one the right length. She picked up a hammer laying on the bench and returned to the bedroom. Using the hammer, she tapped the piece of wood into place between the top of the frame and the top of the lower half of the window.

"No one will be able to open that from the outside now, but if you need to, just tap it with the hammer and it should fall out."

"You think I have a problem, don't you?"

"I think I'm not willing to risk your safety while I find out if you have a problem. If the investigation turns up anything, I'll tell you."

Sondra nodded.

Steph slid into the cruiser and radioed dispatch that she was back in service. She only had one more night on patrol and she would take advantage of it. Most weeknights were fairly quiet, and she would be able to focus on this area. The crackle of her radio interrupted her thoughts.

"Dispatch, two zero five."

She keyed her microphone. "Two zero five, go ahead dispatch."

"Can you check out a disturbance at Fifteen Main Street? Alcohol involved."

"Ten-four."

Fifteen Main Street was Jo's Garage. Steph flipped on her emergency lights again. Jo wouldn't contact the police unless it was something she couldn't handle on her own, and there were few things that fell into that category. Within seconds, she screeched to a stop in front of the middle roll-up door of Jo's business. She unsnapped her holster as she slid from the car. The lights were out upstairs and downstairs, but she could hear voices coming from the rear of the shop. She slowly walked around the building, one hand resting on the butt of her pistol.

Jo stood with her arms crossed watching a middle-aged man in blue jeans and a T-shirt attempting to climb the stairs to her apartment above the garage. Steph stepped beside her and spoke softly.

"That your date for the night?"

Jo grimaced. "I can do better than that."

She laughed. "How'd he get here?"

"I found him sitting on the steps when I closed up for the night. I tried to steer him back to the street, but he becomes a little combative when touched."

She watched him bounce off both handrails as he tried to raise his foot to reach the next step. "He's going to fall down the stairs backward."

"That's what I was afraid of too. Or I might have just gone to bed and left him out here."

"Wait. Is that Billy Ryan?"

"Yep."

"Did you call Kendra? Let her come fight with him."

Jo shrugged. "I wasn't sure if that was a good idea since he was combative."

"He drinks a lot, but I don't remember ever having a call to their house. I've heard she keeps him in line. I don't want to have to fight or arrest him." She used her cell phone to call dispatch. If she arrested him it would be in the papers tomorrow, but she could save him the embarrassment if Kendra took him home. She waited on the line while dispatch dialed Billy's house. When Kendra answered, dispatch patched her through.

"Hey, Kendra. It's Steph Williams."

"What's up, Steph?"

"I have Billy over here at Jo's Garage and I was wondering if you would want him at home or if I should take him to the sheriff's office. He's a little intoxicated."

"That dumbass. I'll come get him."

Kendra hung up without saying good-bye.

"She's coming to get him," Steph relayed to Jo as they watched Billy's boot-covered foot hang in midair while he searched for the next step, the handrails keeping him centered and upright.

Kendra arrived within minutes, Billy having only missed his house by about two blocks. Steph met her in the parking lot and they walked around the garage together. Kendra was a few inches taller than Billy, but her wide frame certainly gave her the advantage.

"Billy! Bring your ass down those steps right now!" Kendra called as soon as she saw where he was.

"Baby," Billy slurred. "I'm trying to get home. I'm late, but I'll be there in just a minute." He turned back to the stairs with renewed vigor and continued to climb.

"Billy Ryan! Do not take another step."

"I got an idea," Steph said as she moved underneath the stairs. She jumped and caught the braces on the back of the deck, pulling herself onto the boards. Climbing the rest of the way, she rolled under the porch railing and onto the deck. She stood and walked to the stairway, looking down at Billy.

"Billy. This is not your house. Turn around and follow Kendra."

Billy looked up in surprise, and Kendra closed the gap to him. Placing her hand on his back, she kept him from toppling over backward.

"This isn't my house?" Billy slurred.

"No, baby. This is not our house." Kendra laced her arm through Billy's and began pulling him back down the stairs.

He went willingly at first, but then he yanked his arm from Kendra's grasp.

"I can do it myself," he said, falling against the handrails.

Kendra took his arm again. "No, you can't. Look at me, Billy. I'm going to help you down the steps and then we can go home."

"Okay. I'm late so I gotta hurry. Kendra will be mad."

Kendra rolled her eyes at Steph but didn't try to convince him differently. At the bottom of the stairs, Billy took his first steps without the handrails to hold him up and fell over backward. His flailing arms collided with Steph, knocking her into the handrail.

"Shit." She pushed Billy back into a standing position and followed him and Kendra around the garage to their car. With Billy safely lying across the backseat, Kendra climbed into the driver's seat.

"I'll follow you and help get him in the house," Steph called as Kendra shut her door.

"Meet you at the diner in ten?" Jo asked her.

She nodded, quickly sliding into her cruiser and following Kendra's car. Kendra wasted no time getting home and dragging Billy from the car. She remained at a distance and let Kendra walk him into the house. Once he was facedown on the couch, she returned to the diner.

"Oh, man. You're gonna have a shiner," Jo said when Steph slid onto the bench across from her.

She touched the tender spot on her cheek. "Shit."

"Hey, Doc. We need an ice pack over here," Jo called to the woman behind the counter. Sally Hamrick, the owner of the diner, turned to look at Jo and Steph.

"What the hell happened to you?" she asked as she moved around the counter and stepped over to their table.

Steph forced herself to remain still while Sally tilted her chin up toward the light. She groaned when Sally gently touched the sore spot below her eye.

"That's a beautiful blue you're sporting. What happened?" Sally asked again.

"She tangled with Billy Ryan," Jo explained.

"Geez, what did Billy do now?"

"He was drunk and missed his apartment by about two blocks. What do you think, Doc? Will she live?"

Steph tried to glare at Jo from the corner of her eye.

"I don't feel any obvious damage. You should have it X-rayed, but I know you won't." Sally released Steph's chin. "I'll get you some ice."

"Now that you've been examined by a veterinarian, do you feel better?" Jo teased.

"Retired veterinarian," Sally countered as she tossed the bag of ice across the counter and onto their table.

"Nice throw, Doc," Steph called as she held the bag to her cheek.

"You guys want some food?"

"Grilled cheese and tomato soup, please," Jo responded first.

"That works for me too," Steph added.

Jo lowered her voice. "I heard Ms. Rivers is selling everything?"

"That's what she says."

"Well, that would certainly suck for Agnes and Kim."

"Yeah. She says she'll try to find someone who will continue to rent to them."

"So she's going to decline the developer's big money?"

Cringing, she dropped the ice pack onto the table. She knew that damn realtor looked too happy earlier. "I didn't know she had an offer already."

"Yeah. Richard's wife was in earlier and she said he was all excited about the offer."

"I guess the money is all they can see."

"They just moved here a couple of months ago. I'm sure someone will set them straight about Agnes and Kim."

"So, what convinced Ms. Rivers to make sure the new owners would keep the tenants? I heard she was only interested in selling and getting out of town."

What had convinced her? Was it that kiss? She thought about the kiss and how good Jemini had felt in her arms. "Agnes bullied her."

Jo laughed. "That's hard to see."

"It was for me too and I was there."

Sally arrived with their food, setting plates and bowls in front of them. She added glasses of water and a cup of coffee for Steph. "Need anything else?"

"We're good. Thanks, Doc."

"You guys talking about how to make that luscious beauty stay in Riverview?" Sally took a step back and leaned against the table behind her.

"You want to work your charm on her, Doc?" Jo asked. "Maybe you can convince her to stay."

Steph felt her face grow warm. She liked Sally, but the thought of anyone touching Jemini made her blood boil.

"I have some charms left, smartass. I might be retired, but I'm not dead."

"What do you think, Steph? Should we risk a bet?" Jo teased.

"Jemini doesn't want to stay in Riverview."

"When did she become Jemini?" Jo raised her eyebrows.

"I think someone else was working their charms. I can't compete with the deputy." Sally sashayed behind the counter.

Steph tried to keep her voice even but the sarcasm still squeezed out in her words. "We already knew she preferred her life in Tennessee to Riverview. She didn't have time for us before Dorothy died, so she's certainly not going to have time for us now."

Jo held up her hands. "Truce. I didn't mean to hit a nerve. She can sell it and move on for all I care. As long as Agnes and Kim have a place to stay."

"Yeah." Steph dropped her gaze to her food. Suddenly she wasn't hungry anymore. She wrapped the sandwich in a napkin to take with her and took a few bites of the soup. Her stomach churned. She didn't want Jemini to be on her way. She wanted Jemini to stay. No, she wanted Jemini to want to stay.

Jo dropped her spoon into her empty bowl. "I'm going to head home. Thanks for clearing my path." After dropping some cash on the table, she waved to Sally and was gone.

Steph added cash to Jo's stack and hurried out behind her. She didn't want Sally to see she hadn't eaten her soup or that she was taking her sandwich to go. The diner was the local center for gossip, and she didn't want to be the topic of conversation. Everyone already knew way too much about her personal life already. The last thing she needed was for anyone to pick up on how she felt about Jemini.

She swung by the sheriff's office and filled out an incident report for the call to Jo's garage. She didn't include Billy Ryan's name, hoping to keep the gossipers at bay a while longer. If she knew Kendra, though, and she did, the story would probably be all over town by morning. She tracked down the other deputy on duty and filled him in about her plans to watch the Pace house throughout the night in between her patrols.

As she approached the edge of town, she noticed a familiar black Mercedes pulled to the side of the road. Recognizing the license plate, she dropped the cruiser into park and took a deep breath. She could wait here until Jemini was safely back in her car. Or she could go and find her. She turned off the engine and stared at the orange and yellow sky.

Would Jemini be happy to see her? Probably not, but she'd take the chance anyway. The last rays of sunlight were fading fast, so she pulled her flashlight from its spot beside her seat. She moved softly through the bushes, following the well-worn trail leading to the rusty iron trestle bridge. A few years ago, the city had declared it a historic landmark and paid to reinforce the supports holding it up. The wooden planks creaked as she stepped up onto the bridge. She could see Jemini about halfway across, leaning on the railing, her forearms supporting her weight as she gazed off into the distance. Her thick, dark curly hair fell around her face and she brushed it back with a finger.

Steph walked down the wooden planks, moving closer to her before speaking. "Thinking about jumping?"

Jemini turned at the sound of her voice and smiled. "Not today, Deputy."

She leaned on the railing beside Jemini, feeling the heat from Jemini's body against her side. The feeling of holding Jemini in her arms was still fresh in her mind. What if she did it again? Would Jemini resist this time?

"I was remembering the time Dorothy brought us up here and let us swing from the rope under the bridge." Jemini's voice was soft and husky with sadness.

"That was fun." She leaned her shoulder into Jemini's, wanting to wipe away any sad memories. "My mom was furious with her for letting us swing on that old rope."

"Until you told her that Dorothy had tested it first."

"Remember the way Dorothy screamed?" Steph asked as the smooth sound of Jemini's laughter joined hers. She would never forget that cloudy day so many years ago. It was one of her final memories of the time before Jemini left. It hadn't been long after Jemini's father's funeral and Dorothy had been sad. It wasn't the last time she and Dorothy had swung out over the riverbed, but she knew better than to mention that to Jemini, especially at this moment.

"What happened to the river?" Jemini asked.

"There were a lot of different contributors, but I think the main one was the rerouting of the flow for the crops up north. From most of the old pictures, it was never a really big river to begin with."

"It just seems strange for Riverview to have no river."

"That's because it wasn't named after a river."

Jemini shrugged. "Yeah, Kathleen was telling me that my ancestors had something to do with it."

"They did. And Dorothy contributed too. She was on every board the town created. From Christmas decorations to a committee for the advancement of Riverview. They even considered changing the name of the town a few years ago, but it never gained any momentum."

"I'm afraid to ask what the suggestions were."

"Nothing good." She stepped away from the railing as the last remaining rays faded in the sky. "Shall we go?"

She pulled her flashlight from the ring on her belt and took Jemini's hand. It felt natural, and she held it a little tighter when Jemini didn't pull away. The glow from the flashlight cast eerie shadows around the path as they walked. When they reached Jemini's car, she clicked the light off. Jemini turned toward her, and she couldn't nor did she want to stop her hand from stroking her soft cheek. She felt her lean into the touch. She wanted to kiss her. Oh, how she wanted to kiss her. The effects from their earlier kiss still lingered and she could still taste the sour candy. Her heart raced as she took a step closer, pressing Jemini into the side of the car. Jemini's hands spread across her back, pulling her even closer. Time stood still as their lips met. She inhaled the sweet smell of lavender, forgetting the fact that she was standing beside the road until the radio microphone attached to her shoulder crackled and dispatch sent the other deputy on duty out on a call.

She stepped back, knowing she needed to put distance between them, or things would move faster than she wanted. She was barely able to resist the feel of Jemini's body under her hands again.

"I guess I should go." Jemini's words sounded reluctant, and Steph wished she could say no.

"Right. Me too."

Jemini quickly opened her door and slid inside the car. Steph took another step back, pushing the door closed and leaning on the open window frame.

"Good night, Deputy." Jemini tapped the gas and the Mercedes pulled back onto the road.

Steph watched the taillights disappear before climbing into her cruiser. She was a little shocked at her own behavior. Never had she kissed a woman while on duty and certainly never like that. She seemed to have no resistance to Jemini. Even now she longed to feel her again. She made a U-turn, driving back toward town. She hoped Jemini was headed back to Lake View for another night. She had forgotten to ask, but she knew she couldn't follow her to find out. She had to be patient and give Jemini room to make her own decisions. She radioed dispatch that she would be making a swing through town before heading again to the Pace residence.

CHAPTER EIGHT

Jemini pulled to the side of the road and rested her head against the steering wheel. Her lips felt hot and bruised. She couldn't believe how easily she had given in to Stephanie's touch again. She prided herself on always maintaining control, but she had to admit Stephanie had been calling all the shots. It was bit unnerving that she and Stephanie couldn't carry on a conversation without arguing or kissing.

Why had Stephanie kissed her again? Maybe she shouldn't lay all the blame on her. She had to admit that she had wanted to feel Stephanie's lips on hers again. She hadn't been able to think about anything else since that moment. There was no way that she was the first woman Stephanie had ever kissed. Could there be a future for them together? She sighed. There would be no future if they couldn't talk. Stephanie had to tell her what happened after she left all those years ago. They had to clear the air between them before they could move forward.

The truth was she had spent her whole life searching for what Stephanie had just made her feel. Most women, even

Robin, were comfortable companions, but there was never the physical connection. Stephanie's kiss evoked feelings in her she couldn't even describe. *Stephanie.* She sighed again. Too bad their paths had led them to this point. She would never see her again once the house was sold.

* * *

Steph parked several blocks away from the Pace residence and dialed Sondra. She told her she would be outside periodically through the night but to call dispatch immediately if she heard anything. She attached an earpiece to her radio, turning the volume down low and quietly left her cruiser. She made a wide circle first and then moved in closer, making sure there was no one around the house. She settled quietly onto one of the chairs on the back porch.

The night was still and warm and she allowed herself to decompress from the day. Leaning her head against the back of the chair, she tried to identify the sounds of the night animals as they settled in around her. The chirp of a cricket or a toad. The occasional screech of a night owl on the prowl for food. She didn't have any doubt that if someone tried to come close to the house, she would be able to tell when the sounds around her went silent.

She replayed her memories with Jemini like a movie in her mind. The earlier unexpected kiss and then tonight's intentional one. She could feel Jemini pulling her closer and responding with fervor. The way Jemini's lips had felt against her own was a sensation she had never experienced. It made her head spin.

She shook off her sudden craving for the taste of Cherry Sours candy. She had to be realistic about this. Jemini lived in Chattanooga and she didn't want to move to Riverview. It seemed there was nothing Steph could do to change her mind. She reminded herself that Jemini had a life in another town. One that possibly included a partner. It seemed unlikely a woman as beautiful as she was would be alone. Until today, she might have believed that partner was a male, but after their kiss, she was pretty sure they had at least one thing in common.

She glanced at her watch. She needed to move before she fell asleep. Apparently whoever had made the tracks around Sondra's house wasn't going to show his or her face tonight. She moved silently off the porch and circled the house as she had when she approached over two hours ago. No sign of anyone. Next time she would come in the early hours of the morning. She had hoped to catch a teenager looking for a peep show, but someone who came after the members of the house were asleep was only looking for trouble.

She rubbed her face as she slid behind the wheel. Her car smelled like grilled cheese. She unwrapped the sandwich, eating half of it. At the convenience store, she threw out the remaining grilled cheese and picked up a fresh cup of coffee. As an afterthought while standing at the checkout counter, she grabbed a bag of Cherry Sours. She wasn't sure she could eat them, but her mouth watered at the thought. She made another pass through town and around Sondra Pace's residence before returning to her office.

The old stone building housed the Riverview City Council as well as the Sheriff's Department. At night the doors were locked and there was no receptionist in the lobby, so she used her key to open the front door. With only two deputies on this shift, it was quiet in the building. She went straight to her office, dropped the bag of candy on her desk, and sat down, pulling the first file from the stack in front of her. She had about two hours left on her shift and without interruption she would be able to clear this entire stack.

When for the third time in an hour she found herself staring at the bag of candy instead of the open file in front of her, she reached out and pulled the bag toward her, ripping the cellophane open. She popped a bright red ball in her mouth and shivered at the sour taste as her teeth crunched the hard candy shell. *How does Jemini eat this crap?* She took a sip of coffee, hoping to wash the taste out of her mouth, but it only made it worse. She grabbed a spare toothbrush from her desk and went into the bathroom where she scrubbed her teeth. She made a fresh pot of coffee, pouring herself a cup without sugar or creamer, and savored the bitter taste.

She dropped the bag of candy on a coworker's desk, where they would be better appreciated, and left the building. Tonight she was not going to be productive, so she would drive around until her shift ended. As she passed the path to the old railroad trestle, she realized her thoughts of Jemini were no longer of the bugs and ice cream of the past, but passionate, heart-stopping kisses and images of muscular legs with smooth, soft brown skin. She was happy when she heard the next shift radio dispatch that they were on duty and she radioed that she was headed home. She fell into bed, her clothes in a pile on the floor, her last thought the taste of sour cherry in her mouth and the feel of Jemini's lips on hers.

* * *

Jemini carried her suitcase and laptop out to her car. She had placed them in the backseat of her Mercedes when Kathleen appeared beside the porch.

"I've been watching for you," Kathleen explained. "Do you mind?"

"Of course not." Jemini was surprised at her answer and even more surprised that it was true. She had enjoyed their walks and was looking forward to having her private sounding board again this morning. She did worry about Kathleen's relationship with Stephanie, and she didn't want to disclose that they had kissed. Not only once but twice in the same day. "I need to get on the road soon."

"Do I hear a 'but' coming," Kathleen asked.

"But." She smiled as Kathleen guided their steps toward the lakeside path. "I wanted to talk with you first. I met Agnes yesterday and she didn't seem happy to have me around."

"That's strange since she told Steph to convince you to stay."

"She did?"

"Yes, I've been told it was what Dorothy wanted."

Jemini took a deep breath. *Why would Dorothy want that?* Twenty years ago, Dorothy's words to her mom had been clear. She could live any lifestyle she chose but not under her roof.

Being a lesbian wasn't something Dorothy would approve of even if it meant losing her granddaughter and surrogate daughter.

"Why would the woman who kicked us out want me to come back?" she finally asked. She wished she could but she didn't expect Kathleen to be able to answer that question.

"She kicked you out?"

This was the conversation she should be having with Stephanie but hadn't been able to. Now that she was pretty sure Stephanie had been living a secret lesbian life that Dorothy hadn't known about, she wondered if she would ever be able to tell her the truth. Stephanie would be crushed as she and her mother had been. She knew she had piqued Kathleen's curiosity, but this conversation would get personal way too quickly. She answered as vaguely as possible. "Well, technically my mother was kicked out and I went along for the ride." She paused for a second before switching topics. "The real estate agent has an offer for the house."

"A buyer already?" Kathleen asked, letting Jemini steer the conversation.

"Yes, but unfortunately it's a developer, and he wants to tear down Dorothy's house for a shopping mall. I'm going to tell him I'm not interested. I still want to sell, but it's only going to be to someone that will allow the tenants to stay."

"That's kind of you and it will be good for Agnes and Kim. I'm a little disappointed, though."

Jemini glanced at her in surprise.

"I thought maybe you would move here and I could have a friend."

"A friend?"

"Well, a friend of my own. Everyone I know here is friends of Cassie."

"Right, you haven't lived here very long?"

Kathleen sighed. "Almost a year. I came for the summer to supervise four girls for the City to Country program and never left. Chase had witnessed a murder and Greg brought him to stay with Cassie right before we arrived. I already liked Cassie but seeing her in that role told me what an honest and sincere person she was. I fell in love immediately and didn't want to leave."

"Wait, did you just say Chase had witnessed a murder? That little boy I saw yesterday morning?"

"He was in the Alabama foster system and had been placed with a husband and wife that were selling drugs. The dealer came after his money and made an example out of the husband. Chase was watching from his bedroom and then hid in his closet until they left."

"Wow, that's crazy. I thought I dealt with bad cases in Chattanooga. Is he doing okay?"

"He is. He and Cassie go to counseling every week. Cassie is great with him. Even Steph spent a lot of time with him last fall. Oh, I didn't mention that the dealer sent a thug to kill Chase after Greg brought him here."

"Here at the farm? Your life has been like a television show."

Kathleen nodded. "Chase led the murderer into the woods. It took Cassie and Steph along with the sheriff's department and a search and rescue team most of the night to find him. That might have been the moment I knew I was never going to leave. When he was missing, I couldn't think right. Then Cassie went to look for him and I didn't have either of them. Thank goodness for Shelley, Dillon's wife. Dillon is our full-time cowboy. Shelley helped me put things in perspective about Cassie. I already knew in my heart that I was attached. I just didn't know how much or how to move forward."

"Wasn't it hard to leave your job and life behind? What about friends?"

"I didn't have any close friends to walk away from. I do miss my job sometimes, but I have enough going on with Chase and Greg. Occasionally I hear from some of the kids that I took care of back then. Honestly, my life with Cassie is everything I could have ever wanted. She is a wonderful woman."

"But your life is not your own." Jemini grimaced. "I didn't mean that to sound as horrible as it did. I only meant that you gave up everything to run this resort with Cassie. Don't you miss the life you worked so hard to create?"

"I understand what you're asking and the answer is no. I have everything I could ever want here. I could've kept my career and traveled to Pensacola for work. But why? I love waking up every day with Cassie and the life we share. I can't imagine being anywhere else."

Jemini struggled to make Kathleen's words match her own life. Could she be happy in Riverview with Stephanie? Or without her? Her career had always been her life and she had worked hard to be where she was. Could she give it all up?

"I hope that no matter what happens you will still visit," Kathleen said with a smile.

"I'd like that. This place is beautiful and I've enjoyed your company too."

"What has Steph said about your decision to sell?"

"*I want something more permanent.*" Stephanie's words echoed through her mind. Did Stephanie really want something more permanent? And did she want it with her? She couldn't really think about that right now. Maybe she could hope for a chance to have a real conversation with Stephanie. One that involved talking.

"She only cared that I was still selling the house and I didn't get a chance to tell her that I would make sure the new owner would allow the tenants to stay."

Jemini had guided their walk back toward her car. She needed to get on the road if she wanted to have time to talk with Karen before the hearing.

"Maybe you can tell her tonight. You'll be back for the cookout, right?" Kathleen asked.

"I'm going to try. My hearing is at one so unless the judge has a lot to say we should be out of there by two."

"Whatever time you get here will be fine. I'm just glad you're coming back."

She was too. She only hoped that Stephanie would be glad too.

* * *

Jemini tried to feel excited about returning home, but even the view of Chattanooga in the distance didn't seem as welcoming as it normally did. The city that she called home seemed cold and foreign to her today. Chattanooga had been the first big town she and her mother had come to the day they left Dorothy's house. It had felt so large to her that day after being in Riverview. When her mother asked if she wanted to stay here, she had said yes. There were plenty of mountains and trees surrounding Chattanooga. Everything a young tomboy could want. Except her best friend.

She had made new friends but never allowed them to get as close as Stephanie had been. In the back of her mind, she was always waiting for her mother to decide it was time to move again. She knew her heart couldn't take that kind of a loss for a second time. She had picked up and dropped friends like the rocks in her backyard, never holding onto one for any period of time.

The little house with the yard her mother had found for them had been perfect, but as soon as she graduated from college she'd found an apartment in the heart of the city. Her body had craved something different from Riverview. She wanted the old brick and steel buildings to surround her. To feel their strength and power in her life every day. When she finally had enough money to search for something better to call her own, she went straight for the cold edges of the city's modern steel condos. There was no doorman there to remember her name each night when she came home from work, only an electronic scanner that recognized her keycard. There was no one to say good-bye to each morning. And no one to break her heart when they left.

Her condominium was located on the tenth floor of a fifteen-story building. Walking around its sparsely decorated rooms, she tried to spot something that made it feel like home. It just felt cold and lonely. She wondered if other people saw her life that way as well. Would Stephanie?

She was tired of being alone, Jemini decided. She wanted someone to fill the emptiness in her life. Someone she could trust to share her life. She didn't know, though, if Stephanie was the one who could fill that void. Or if she would even want to try.

It was crazy how solid her life had seemed barely a week ago, everything moving along smoothly until the call from Mr. Cross changed it all. She no longer felt comfortable here. The strangest part for her was how many times in the last couple of days she had insisted she could not leave this life. What exactly was she holding on to? She wasn't really sure anymore. As she filled her suitcase with clean clothes, she steadfastly avoided thinking about how long she planned to stay in Riverview. She quickly grabbed her bags and returned to her car.

The drive from her condo to her office was less than two miles, but early afternoon traffic was out in full force. She was able to avoid the heavy congestion on Interstate 24 and deal with only local traffic once she got to Georgia Avenue. Hanging her permit from the mirror, she found a parking spot in the garage beneath the courthouse. The prestigious law office of Thompson, Myers, and Rivers was located just across the street. In fact, she could look out her office window and into one of the many offices assigned to county judges.

She was waved around the metal detector on the first floor and headed straight to the elevator. She'd only been away for a day, but since she'd never missed a day before and was around most weekends, the security staff at the office appeared to feel the need to welcome her back. She exited the elevator on the eighth floor and gave a wave to the firm's receptionist, who was engaged with a client on the phone.

"It's about damn time," Karen exclaimed when Jemini strolled into her office.

"I missed you too, Karen."

"Everything you need for this afternoon is on your desk. After your hearing, I thought we'd go over your schedule for next week."

"I'm heading back to Riverview as soon as the hearing is over."

Karen followed her into her office, sinking into the c' across from her. "Okay. When are you coming back?"

"I'm not sure." She hesitated for a second, not sure how Karen would take her next words. "What if I said I'm not?"

In a way she was as shocked as Karen at her words, but if she thought about it she knew the town of Riverview was calling to her. She couldn't have been more wrong when she said she didn't have any emotional ties to Riverview. She wasn't sure when she had started contemplating moving there, but it seemed now like the idea had always been there. In the past, she had always worked hard to push those thoughts away but with the option right in front of her, she was finding it hard not to jump at the possibility.

"What does that mean?"

Jemini sunk into her desk chair and rubbed her face. "I'm not sure. Would you think I was crazy if I said returning to Riverview felt like coming home?"

"Maybe not crazy, but maybe it's just your emotions getting the best of you. You've had a tough week. I don't remember you ever mentioning or visiting your grandmother before. Were you close to her?"

"We haven't been close since I was a kid, but the house and the people have brought back a lot of memories."

"You're a partner here. It's not like Ken or Keith would have anything to say about you taking time off. Take as much time as you want to explore your past, and I'll hold down the fort while you're gone."

"Thanks, Karen." Jemini smiled. "If I did leave, would you consider coming with me?"

Karen's eyes widened. "To Riverview?"

"Yes."

She felt Karen searching her face for answers she wasn't sure she even had for herself. After a few moments, Karen stood. At the door she stopped without turning around, and her voice, soft and a bit unsure, floated back into the room. "I would."

* * *

Jemini strolled through the hospital and located the staff oom. She had one more stop that she needed to make before she was ready to turn her attention to her case and their appearance before Judge Stevens. Even though the hospital was around the corner from her office, she had never before taken the time to visit Robin at work. One more sign that they had never really connected. She found Robin exactly where the nurse at the emergency room desk had said she would be. She was sitting with her head on the table and a can of Mountain Dew in front of her.

"Hey," she said, gently touching Robin's shoulder.

Robin raised her head and looked at her with red-rimmed eyes. "You're back."

There was no excitement in Robin's voice. "Rough night?" she asked, staring at the woman she had called her girlfriend for the last several months.

"Rough two nights. I went out with Mary on my night off and the hospital was hopping last night. This is the first break I've had. It's a full moon, you know."

She smiled, hoping to soften the blow of her words. "I'm heading back to Riverview tonight, but I wanted to tell you I might not be back for a while."

Robin shrugged. "Okay. So, that's it then. I'll leave your key when I get my stuff out of the condo."

She almost took a step backward. Robin's words weren't condemning, but their finality was harsh. She had thought she would break things off with her when she returned and she certainly hadn't expected Robin's easy response. "You're okay with this?"

"I didn't expect it to last forever. We're pretty different. It was fun, though. Let me know if you want to hook up when you come back." Robin dropped her head back on the table, ending their conversation.

She shook her head even though Robin wasn't looking at her. She knew she would never call Robin again. No matter what happened with Stephanie in Riverview.

She quickly crossed the street and cleared the metal detector to enter the courthouse. The meeting wasn't in a courtroom, but the judge's chambers were located on a secure floor in the same building. She found her clients and their two children waiting in the hallway and ushered them inside. Judge Stevens's chamber was small and barely had room for the two chairs and the couch. The kids were now snuggled between their parents; she hoped they would all be going home together today.

"That's not right!" Dennis Ross, the county prosecutor exclaimed as he entered the room. "They need to be separated until a decision is made."

"Shut up, Dennis," she said, standing. "They haven't seen their parents in almost two weeks."

"They saw them when they ran away three days ago."

Thankfully the judge walked in before she had to respond to his stupidity. The court reporter followed him and took his seat at the recording machine.

"Thanks to everyone for meeting here today. Go around the room and state your names for the record."

"Jemini Rivers. Counsel for the defense."

"Dennis Ross. For the State."

"Gloria Watson. Defendant."

"Donald Watson. Defendant."

Judge Stevens looked at both boys and nodded.

"Tyler Watson."

"Donnie Watson."

"Excellent. I'm Judge Stevens. I'll be presiding over today's hearing," he continued. "I've called everyone here to get this case cleared up and off my docket. Ms. Rivers, can you give us a summary for the record?"

"Yes, sir. On January twenty-seventh, Donnie Watson was taken to the hospital for a broken arm and two weeks later he returned to have the same arm set again. As per Tennessee law, the hospital nurse filled out the paperwork to have the Watsons' case checked for child abuse. Before the investigation could be started, Tyler Watson was admitted overnight for multiple contusions and a concussion. On February fifth, the case finally made it under review and both children were removed from the home. The Watsons hired Thompson, Myers, and Rivers, and the case was placed on my desk. We appealed the removal of the children from the home and I began filing to have the children returned immediately."

"You have documentation for the injuries?"

"Partially, sir. Donnie was alone when he fell from his tree house." She glanced at the little blond-haired boy. "Twice. I have documentation from Tyler's football coach concerning his injuries, though."

Judge Stevens removed his glasses. "Mr. and Mrs. Watson, can you step out of the room for a moment?"

Everyone waited silently as they hugged their boys and left the room. Judge Stevens motioned the boys to come forward. Jemini stood with them, guiding them closer to his desk.

"Can I see that arm?" Judge Stevens asked.

Donnie proudly held up his cast.

"You don't have very many signatures. Can I sign it?"

Donnie nodded eagerly, laying his arm across Judge Stevens's desk. Across the top of the cast Judge Stevens wrote "The Judge" and Donnie giggled.

"Tell me about your tree house," Judge Stevens encouraged.

"It's in the biggest tree in the backyard. Dad helped me build it. Tyler says I'm a sissy because it's not very high off the ground, but it's farther than it looks."

Judge Stevens nodded. "How did you break your arm?"

"Mom called me for dinner. I was hurrying and my foot slipped."

"And the second time?"

"My shoestring caught and I couldn't climb up or down. I couldn't yell for help because Mom and Dad told me I wasn't allowed in my tree house until the cast came off." He shrugged. "All my favorite stuff is up there."

Judge Stevens smiled and addressed Tyler. "And you're a football player?"

"Yes, sir."

"I played football myself, but I don't remember getting any bruises like that." He pointed at the pictures of Tyler's bruised stomach and ribs.

Tyler hung his head. "I got in a fight after practice."

"A fight, huh. Tell me what happened, son."

"Some of the guys were mouthing off about how we suck and they said they let the defense sack our quarterback on purpose."

"So you took on the entire offensive line?" Judge Stevens smiled at Jemini.

"Kinda."

"All right, boys. Take your seats. Bring the parents back in."

She squeezed both boys' shoulders as she opened the door and motioned for Gloria and Donald to come back in. She gave them an encouraging nod.

She glanced at Dennis, surprised but pleased that he had remained quiet throughout the hearing.

"I find that Tyler and Donnie Watson should be returned to their home. The state will continue to monitor for up to one year after the last incident including any future injuries that may occur." He addressed Donald and Gloria. "It's in your best interest to report all injuries to your case worker immediately."

"The state would like to continue in-home inspections for the duration the case is open, Your Honor," Dennis requested.

Allowing in-home inspections meant a caseworker could appear at the Watsons' door at any time day or night and had to be allowed access to the house and the boys. This implied Donald and Gloria were guilty and would make for a very unpleasant year for the entire family.

Jemini started to protest, but Judge Stevens made a motion to silence her.

He rubbed his forehead before turning to face Dennis. "I understand your request and in most cases I would agree. Personally, I think this was all an unfortunate situation. Let's let this family return to their lives."

She could tell Dennis was upset, but she couldn't help but smile. This was why she did her job; it made everything worthwhile when justice prevailed. She hadn't expected Judge Stevens to clear them completely, but apparently he had reviewed all the material sent over by her office.

"Thank you, Your Honor," she said as she motioned the Watson family into the hallway.

Gloria surprised her with a hug and she readily returned it. Donald and Gloria had been wrongly accused and their case had been easy to fight. Thompson, Myers, and Rivers kept the best investigators on salary. Once they were finished digging into every corner, she took the analysis of all the information discovered and if she doubted the defendant's claims she would not take their case. She might work for the underdog, but it was always the innocent underdog.

CHAPTER NINE

Steph pulled into Lake View, her eyes instantly searching for Jemini's car. Her heart sank when she didn't see it parked outside her cabin. It was hard for her to believe that Jemini had taken the developer's offer and then left without a word. Brandon shifted excitedly on the seat beside her. Kathleen had called and suggested she bring him to play with Chase so she had picked him up from school. Kim was invited too when she got off from work, but she had decided to take advantage of a quiet evening alone instead.

As usual Brandon had begun talking as soon as he climbed in her truck. She was surprised to hear he had chatted with Jemini the previous night. She tried to grill him for information, but he was easily distracted, especially the closer they got to Lake View. She finally gave up, discovering nothing more than his opinion that she was nice and would be coming for dinner at some point.

Chase met Brandon at the door of the truck as soon as they parked and the two ran off immediately. They were early for the cookout so she followed the boys toward the lake. Finding a shady bench, she tried to relax. She still couldn't believe Jemini would leave without telling her. She wanted to ask Cassie or Kathleen if they had talked to her, but she knew she couldn't do that without revealing how deep her interest in Jemini really was.

She wasn't ready to put her attraction into words even with her friends. Her mind and body had played tricks on her while she slept and for once she wasn't able to ease her arousal alone. She leaned forward on the bench and put her face in her hands. Jemini had touched more than her body. There was a connection between them. Something bigger than a shared childhood and she wanted to explore it. No, she wanted to embrace it. The problem was they couldn't communicate. They hadn't even been able to manage a normal conversation yet.

There had been plenty of women in her life over the years, especially when she was in college, but none had the effect on her that Jemini did. Her body hummed with anticipation at the thought of seeing her again and she couldn't help but wonder if she would. Brandon's high-pitched squeal made her lift her head and check on the boys. They ran through ankle-deep water at the edge of the lake, chasing each other. Chase's thin pale legs glowed in the sunlight beside the thickness of Brandon's brown calves.

To have fun and play—that was all that mattered to them in this moment, enjoying a friendship that went beyond their differences. She remembered the thrill of having Jemini as a companion and playmate. The contrast in their skin colors had held no significance to them either. Not then anyway. Things had changed a bit in the last twenty years. When her freckles had appeared each summer, Steph had been jealous of Jemini's bronze skin tone. Now, she was painfully aware how very attractive it made her.

"Hey, stranger," Kathleen said, sitting down beside her.

"Hey."

"What are you doing out here alone?"

"I figured you guys were busy getting ready for the cookout, and I didn't want to get in your way."

Kathleen watched the boys before turning her attention back to Steph. "Thanks for bringing Brandon. We've had mostly adults this week and Chase has been pretty lonely."

"Brandon goes to an after-school program when Kim's at work, but I think he ends up doing a lot of babysitting of the younger kids since he's the oldest kid there."

They both laughed when Brandon dove to the ground, kicking sand all over Chase. He stood, spitting sand out of his mouth, and both boys ran into the water to rinse off.

"We'll put them both in the outside shower before dinner," Kathleen suggested.

"That would be great. I can only imagine the places he has sand."

"Makes my skin itch just thinking about it. Are you going to ask about her?" Kathleen let the silence stretch before she prompted her again. "Steph?"

"What am I supposed to say? She left, right?"

She saw Kathleen's eyes widen at the anguish in her voice, and she tried cover it. "I can see her car is gone. I should have expected it. She already has an offer on the house."

"She's only gone for the day. She's planning to come back tonight."

Relief flooded through her. She turned away from Kathleen. She would get another chance to convince Jemini to stay. Later she would worry about how she was going to do that. She had been so unsuccessful to date she couldn't even come up with a plan. She thought about their kisses earlier. Each one said more than she had been able to say in two days. Maybe that was the only way they could communicate. She certainly wouldn't argue about having more of that.

"You like her, right?" Kathleen asked.

"What's not to like? Oh well, aside from the fact she's selling Dorothy's house from underneath Agnes and Kim."

"Come on, Steph. You know this isn't easy for her."

Steph ran a hand across her face, rubbing her eyes. This wasn't easy for her either. She had already decided if Kim and Agnes moved, then she was selling her place too. The house and the property would never bring her peace again. The thought of losing her family's home brought back the anger she hadn't felt in a while.

Her eyes met Kathleen's as the words sank in, reminding her that Kathleen seemed to know more than she should. "You've been talking to her, haven't you?"

"Maybe a little."

Steph raised her eyebrows, waiting for Kathleen to continue.

"She's very confused, but the last time we talked she seemed adamant that she wouldn't sell unless they allowed Agnes and Kim to stay."

"Really? I guess that's a start. I didn't have a lot of confidence in our ability to bring her home like Dorothy wanted anyway."

"I wouldn't give up yet," Kathleen said with a mischievous smile. "I think we should all go out tonight."

"Go out? Like to dinner? But what about the cookout?"

"No, I mean dancing. After dinner. Greg is coming so he can watch the boys. Cassie and I have been talking about going to a lesbian bar in Pensacola for a while."

Maybe a night out and away from Jemini would be just what she needed to clear her head. She shrugged. "Okay."

"Great. I'll ask Jemini when she gets back."

Steph frowned. Inviting Jemini wasn't what she had in mind. Why would Jemini want to go out with them anyway? "With Jemini too? I'm not sure that's her style."

"I think she could use a carefree evening."

"A carefree evening maybe, but I'm not sure she would fit in at a lesbian bar."

"Why not?"

"I'm not sure...I mean...I don't know if she is or not."

"She is."

She glanced at Kathleen and then back at the boys, who were now pushing each other off the floating dock. She forced any emotion from her face. "How do you know that?"

"She told me."

Steph couldn't stop the grin from spreading across her face. She no longer had to feel bad about kissing Jemini. Maybe there were other ways she could convince Jemini to stay in Riverview and maybe, just maybe, she had a chance for something more.

Kathleen grasped her chin and turned her face back toward her. "What happened to your eye?"

"Hazards of the job."

Kathleen gently stroked the bruise on her cheek before dropping her hand. Her displeasure in Steph's job was evident. "I won't ask for details since you already know police work makes me crazy. Cassie doesn't talk much about her law enforcement career so I try not to bring it up either. I'm glad there are men and women willing to do the job, I only wish it wasn't my friends."

"You know I love my job, right?"

"I do and I'm glad, but I'll always worry. Back to the original conversation. So, you do like her then?"

"I like her," she answered without thinking. Kathleen was easy to talk to and this wasn't the first time she had ever revealed more than she wanted to. When she was coming over every evening to interview Chase after his ordeal, she and Kathleen had had long conversations about raising children. As well as her own desire to one day have a child. These were things she would never say to Cassie. As far as anyone else was concerned, she didn't want children or even a spouse to smother her. And mostly that was true. Jemini's entrance into her life had certainly made her start thinking about what her life could be like if she was willing to let someone in.

"So, what do you think about tonight?" Kathleen asked.

"I'm in, if you can convince Jemini."

"Leave that to me," Kathleen said with an evil grin.

* * *

The smile was stuck on Jemini's face as she turned into Lake View and spotted Stephanie's truck. She was later than she had hoped to be and it appeared the cookout was in full swing. There were quite a few people standing around the brick grill, but it only took her a second to locate Stephanie. Her hands in the pockets of her cargo shorts, she was leaning against a nearby picnic table. Her blond hair was in its usual ponytail, and she looked relaxed but she had seen Stephanie turn her head to follow the car's path.

She pulled her eyes away long enough to park her car and then joined the group. She gave Stephanie what she hoped was a casual nod and listened attentively while Kathleen introduced her to the others standing around. Her eyes kept returning to Stephanie and she was pleased to see she was looking at her each time too. She couldn't help but frown when she noticed the discoloration on Stephanie's cheek. Stephanie noticed her looking and shrugged. She took that to mean it wasn't anything serious, but she still had to force herself to resist the urge to check her for additional damage. At the first opportunity to escape politely, she moved away from the group, walking toward the water before she did something to embarrass herself and Stephanie.

During the drive from Chattanooga, she had almost convinced herself that her feelings for Stephanie weren't really as intense as she was feeling, but seeing her again had sent her heart racing. Selling the house was an absolute necessity. She couldn't take care of that much property, and she was pretty sure she didn't want to live in Dorothy's house. However, selling the house didn't mean she couldn't spend time in Riverview. She wasn't sure she was completely serious when she asked Karen if she would be willing to move with her, but the idea was starting to take shape in her mind.

Her gaze drifted to the two boys filling their plates at the table. The heaping piles of food looked ready to fall on both sides. She saw Cassie moving closer to them and she expected her to assist them, but she didn't. Her fingers absently played with Chase's hair when she passed him and he turned to follow her, cradling his plate in both hands. Cassie had confidence in Chase's ability even though he was small and because of that she allowed him the space to be himself. Though Chase still chose to be close to her it was out of love, Jemini could tell, and not because he needed something from her.

Her heart warmed even more when she saw Brandon choose a seat beside Stephanie. It was sweet the way she stopped eating and helped him settle his plate on the table. She passed him the bottle of water Cassie had brought over for them and watched to make sure he could get it open before returning to her own plate. When Brandon wrinkled his nose at something on Stephanie's plate, she offered him a bite. He must have liked it because Stephanie gave him a scoop from her plate.

She had never thought about having children. No one she had dated ever seemed like they would be around long enough to make a family. And then there was her work. She had plenty of surrogate children from her cases but none who would seek her out first as Chase had Cassie. Or even as Brandon had done to Stephanie. She was glad she had broken up with Robin. They had both known there was no future there, and now she could dream about the possibilities. Not that she necessarily wanted children, but she did at least want someone who would welcome her home. She was tired of coming home to the emptiness that haunted her condo.

"Are you hiding from our guests?" Kathleen asked with a smile as she walked toward her.

"Not hiding. Just stretching my legs."

"That's understandable. How was your trip? Other than fast. How long is that drive?"

"About three or four hours, depending which way I go. Through Atlanta is faster, but traffic is heavier. The trip went well and I got everything I asked for from the judge."

"That's great, but speaking of getting everything you asked for, I've been hounding Cassie for weeks for a night out. Would you like to get away for a while tonight?"

"What did you have in mind?"

"Cassie, Steph, and I are going to a lesbian bar in Pensacola."

Jemini's mind froze and she was glad her gaze had been locked on the fountain of water in the middle of the lake in front of her. Could she handle an evening at a dark bar with Stephanie? She wanted to and, really, nothing else mattered. The idea of having an excuse to be close to Stephanie without having to make any decisions for the night was a wonderful thought.

"So, what do you think?" Kathleen asked, reminding her she was still waiting for an answer.

"Sure. It sounds like fun."

"Excellent. We'll leave around eight. Cassie will need a shower after standing over the grill, but she's fast."

"I'll be ready."

Kathleen nodded toward the group. "Ready to join everyone again? The food is getting cold."

She looped her arm through Kathleen's and fell into step beside her. The burgers, hot dogs, and steaks were sitting on a nearby table, and Kathleen left her to fill her plate. She willingly took the empty seat beside Stephanie and listened to her tell police stories. Everyone laughed when she explained what had caused her bruised cheek. She tried to avoid looking at her while they ate, but when her leg accidentally brushed against Stephanie's, she didn't move it. The pressure was comforting and she liked the feel of the heat from touching her thigh. Stephanie didn't seem to mind the contact either. Tonight was going to be interesting.

CHAPTER TEN

Steph hadn't noticed Cassie sneak off to the shower, but she saw her return with wet hair. The cookout was winding down and she watched her moving through the remaining guests as she said goodnight to each of them. She looked down at her cargo shorts and was pleased to see no stains. She was glad she had chosen a blouse rather than a T-shirt. Cassie wore cargo shorts too and when Jemini and Kathleen appeared from the house a few moments later they also wore shorts.

"Ready to go?" Kathleen asked, threading her arm through Steph's.

"How about if I drive my truck?" Steph suggested.

"Oh, I like that idea. I've never been in the backseat with Cassie."

Steph shook her head. "I'll put you both out if you fog up my windows."

Kathleen laughed and slid her other arm through Jemini's as they walked toward Steph's truck.

"Want me to go grab Cassie?" Steph asked when she noticed Cassie was still talking with some guests.

"No, I'll rescue her." Kathleen slid out from between them, placing Jemini's hand on Steph's arm. Jemini didn't pull away, and Steph squeezed her elbow against her body, holding Jemini's hand tightly. When they reached the truck, she pulled open the front passenger door and held it while Jemini climbed inside.

"Wait, I'm not driving?" Cassie stopped at Steph's truck. "We'll be more comfortable in my SUV."

"Just get in, Cassie." Kathleen nudged her. "I want you in the backseat."

Cassie shrugged and climbed in behind Kathleen.

"What were the boys doing when you went in to shower?" Kathleen asked Cassie.

"Greg was making a frozen pizza and the boys already had sheets spread across the living room."

"Sheets?" Jemini asked, turning to look at Cassie and Kathleen.

"Chase likes to make clubhouses out of sheets. That's probably where they'll sleep tonight. It's like a tent," Kathleen explained.

"That sounds like fun." Jemini turned back to the front.

"I'd build you a sheet fort if you come home with me," Steph said softly, hoping only Jemini could hear her. The smile on Jemini's face told her she had. So had the others.

"I'm too old for sleeping on the floor," Cassie moaned.

"I don't think you were invited, sweetheart," Kathleen whispered loudly as she pulled Cassie's arm across her shoulders and snuggled in against her chest.

Steph concentrated on driving and let the others carry the conversation. She was surprised Jemini had agreed to come along and that Kathleen had confirmed she was a lesbian. It was weird because now she wasn't sure how to act around her. She loved the way Jemini had smiled at her flirting comment and she wanted to make it happen again.

The drive to Pink's went quickly as she listened to Jemini and Kathleen talk about their work with children in and out of the foster care system. The laws between Florida and Tennessee seemed comparable as was the number of children being neglected. She maneuvered the truck through the streets filled with Friday night traffic. Pink's was located in an industrial area and was the only building showing any movement at this hour. It had only been open for a couple of years and it catered to both male and female patrons. Lesbian night was Friday; the boys would take over on Saturday. Steph could only remember being here once before. It hadn't been a pleasant night—blind dates almost never were.

The thump-thump of music from the bar bombarded them as they crossed the parking lot. A uniformed security guard walked between the cars, a grim reminder that their sexuality was still a target for any crazy lunatic. The door at the entrance was propped open and a bouncer dressed in black met them as they approached. A 1980s Madonna song blared from behind her as she checked their driver's licenses with a small flashlight. The neon pink lights around the door were the only sign that they might be entering a lesbian bar.

Steph followed her instinct and took Jemini's hand as they followed Cassie and Kathleen inside. She stopped just inside the door behind Cassie as they each took the time to absorb the atmosphere of the room and adjust to the throbbing music. Strobe lights flashed from multiple locations around the dance floor, casting an intermittent glow across the tables. Though the dance floor was already crowded, there were still a few tables open.

Cassie leaned into Steph, speaking loudly. "We'll get a table if you'll grab the first round."

"Beer?"

"Yep."

She glanced at Kathleen and Jemini, yelling over the music. "Beer?"

They both nodded.

She gave Jemini's hand a squeeze before dropping it and heading to the bar. When she was finally able to reach the dark, glossy counter, she stopped and watched Jemini follow Cassie and Kathleen toward an open table. She took a few minutes to savor the idea that tonight she would be allowed to touch Jemini without worrying about the consequences. Being on a dance floor meant the imaginary boundary between them had been lifted. Then tomorrow they could go back to the way things were. The music was so loud she didn't have to worry about saying the wrong thing and driving Jemini farther away. Steph felt her heart race. A part of her wished urgently that they were alone instead of in public. She turned back to the bar and waited her turn to place their drink orders.

* * *

Jemini's eyes scanned the room across the faces and bodies of many women but stopped as they reached Stephanie. She couldn't help but appreciate the way Stephanie carried herself. Her back was always straight with her head held high, but she knew it wasn't a stiff posture. She had felt Stephanie's body pressed against her own and she knew it was soft in all the right places. She couldn't help but like the confidence that radiated through her. She wanted to attribute her attraction to Stephanie to lust, especially the way her blood had boiled each time Stephanie kissed her, but deep down it felt like more. She was eager to get on the dance floor and be wrapped in her embrace. Her eyes quickly found Stephanie still standing at the bar when she felt movement beside her. She glanced at the woman who now occupied Stephanie's seat. Her gaze moved to the fresh bottle of beer on the table in front of her and then to Kathleen's raised eyebrows.

"You looked a little thirsty," the dark-haired woman said, leaning closer to be heard.

"My partner is at the bar getting our drinks."

The woman raised both hands. "No problem." She glanced at Cassie and Kathleen, shrugging. "Can't blame a girl for hitting on the most beautiful woman in the room."

Cassie shook her head, laughing. "Maybe that line will work on someone else tonight."

The woman stood and shrugged again before disappearing into the crowd.

* * *

"What…where?" Steph looked at the drink in front of Jemini as she set the bottles she had bought on the table.

"Someone else was trying to hit on your girl while you were gone," Kathleen teased.

Anger filled Steph as she thought of anyone else touching Jemini. She reminded herself that maybe someone else's advances weren't unwelcome to Jemini. She needed to accept the fact that she might not be the only person dancing with Jemini tonight; she didn't have any right to lay claim to her. She tried to keep the anger out of her voice and the sarcasm slid out instead. "Don't let me interrupt your moves."

"And on that pleasant note, we'll head for the dance floor." Cassie pulled Kathleen to her feet. As she passed behind Steph, she leaned in and whispered, "You should know she turned her down flat."

Steph dropped into the seat beside Jemini. "I'm sorry. Seems my instincts aren't working well tonight."

"It's okay. How are mine? I saw the bartender touch your hand when she gave you your change."

Steph shrugged. "Just being friendly I guess. The music was too loud for words."

Jemini raised an eyebrow before pushing the rejected bottle aside and grabbing one from in front of Steph.

Her breath caught as she watched Jemini place the bottle to her lips and tip it up, taking a long drink. She suddenly found every movement Jemini made erotic and she pulled her eyes away from Jemini's fingers, wet from the moisture on the bottle. She turned to watch Cassie release Kathleen and then pull her close again as the slow song faded into a fast rhythm. She wanted what they had and she was tired of waiting for it to happen. She looked back at Jemini. "I'm not the best dancer, but I'm willing if you are."

Jemini stood, placing her hand in Steph's. "Let's do it."

Though she didn't want to, she released Jemini's hand when they reached the dance floor. The music was even louder here and she closed her eyes trying to feel the rhythm. She felt Jemini step closer as their bodies began to move together. She opened her eyes and connected with Jemini's inches from her own. They were dark and filled with temptations she wasn't sure she had ever experienced. Her body struggled to find the rhythm of the music again. Thankful that the music had drowned out her groan, she tried to pretend Jemini's closeness wasn't having an effect on her. She concentrated on the pounding beat, letting her body move with Jemini as they danced through several fast songs. When a slow song finally made it into the rotation, she hesitated, waiting to see if Jemini would choose to return to their seats.

Jemini didn't miss a beat, sliding into her arms. Overwhelmed by the sensations coursing through her, Steph squeezed her eyes shut again. Jemini's skin was soft. But the muscle beneath was hard. She pulled her tighter, resting her head against Jemini's. Though Jemini's hands roamed up and down her back, sliding in and out of her hip pockets, Steph forced hers to remain still at Jemini's waist. The heavy breaths Jemini was taking when she buried her face in her neck did nothing to prepare her for the gentle wisps she felt as Jemini's breathing slowed to match the music. She inhaled deeply, taking in Jemini's scent. The fresh clean smell was mixed with a light touch of lavender, reminding Steph of the purple flowers growing outside her bedroom window.

* * *

Jemini had fought the urge for as long as she could and now she gently pressed her lips to Stephanie's neck. Little kisses traced a line to her earlobe and back down to the base of her neck. She pulled her head away, quickly reading her face before she began placing kisses on the other side of her neck. Stephanie's eyes were closed, but Jemini was encouraged by the look of rapture on her face. As the end of the song neared, she stopped directly in front of Stephanie's face. She wanted to kiss her and she couldn't think of a single reason not to. *Stephanie.*

Steph. Whichever name she used it still made her feel the same. Sliding her arms up to rest on Steph's shoulders, she played with the wispy pieces of hair that had escaped from her ponytail. When the last note faded, she pulled Steph's head toward her and pressed her lips to Steph's.

There was no hesitation, but she still feared Steph would pull away. When Steph opened her mouth and their tongues met, however, the kiss deepened sending a blast of heat through Jemini's body. She knew this was the passion that she had heard others talk about. The desire for more cascaded into a need she didn't want to quench. Their motion stopped when a hand fell on each of their shoulders.

"The music stopped," Cassie said, her voice filled with laughter.

"Leave them alone," Kathleen chastised.

"I just thought they should know that everyone in the room is watching."

Those words shot through her and she knew Steph would feel them too. Neither wanted to be the object of such attention.

"Sorry," she said, hoping Steph could read her lips.

Steph leaned close to her ear, her arm still wrapped tight around Jemini's body. "Please don't be sorry."

She smiled, leaning into Steph as they followed Cassie and Kathleen back to their table. She wasn't sorry. In fact, she couldn't wait to get Steph back on the dance floor.

Cassie picked up one of the open bottles on their table but quickly set it back down without taking a drink. She looked at Steph. "We need fresh drinks."

"I was thinking the same thing."

"We've got this round," Kathleen said, pulling Jemini to her feet.

She gave Steph a smile before helping Kathleen push their way through the crowd to the bar.

Kathleen managed to find a hole in the people lining the bar and placed their drink orders before turning back to Jemini. "Looks like things are going well between you guys," she said loudly into Jemini's ear.

Things were going well. For the first time since their paths had crossed the night she arrived, Jemini felt a warmth emanating from Steph. The smile that had been stuck on her face since they left the dance floor widened.

"Are you thinking about moving here now?" Kathleen asked.

Jemini felt her smile fade. She really hadn't allowed herself to think about their situation at all tonight. She had just enjoyed being close to Steph.

Kathleen shook her head. "I'm sorry. Please bring the smile back."

"I hadn't thought about reality for the last couple of hours. I do like her, but that's not a reason to move here. Besides she might not feel the same way about me."

"Oh, she feels the same," Kathleen assured her.

Jemini blushed. Kathleen had a way of getting right to the point. "I'm sure she feels the same lust, but it might not go any deeper. Moving here would be presumptuous, I'm afraid."

"Maybe, but that's what talking is for."

Kathleen turned back to the bar as their drinks were set in front of them, handing a few bills to the bartender with a nod to keep the change.

"We're not very good at that," Jemini said under her breath. She and Steph had yet to have a conversation that didn't involve Steph getting angry or storming off. Normally, she could feel the underlying tension between them when they were close, but tonight had been all about having fun. Maybe they could talk tonight while they were both still riding high from the excitement.

Jemini carried two of the bottles as they pushed their way through the crowd back to the table. She couldn't stop her smile from returning when she met Steph's gaze. She felt almost giddy with the thrill of attraction. She couldn't help but think about what it would be like to have Steph's hands on her body again. The thought of them touching her skin and running across her breasts made her pulse race.

"Do you want to dance some more?" Steph asked, leaning close.

She nodded eagerly. She was back in her fantasy world. Plus she couldn't wait to get her hands back on Steph's body.

"Let us know when you guys are ready to leave," Steph called to Cassie and Kathleen as they stood.

"Not just yet," Kathleen called back. "I want to dance some more."

Steph nodded, leading Jemini back to the dance floor.

* * *

Her legs aching, Jemini accepted Steph's hand to help her into the truck. She had caressed every inch of Steph's body that could be considered acceptable in public, but she now longed to touch the areas blocked by clothing. She no longer had any doubts about Steph's attraction to her, but her insecurities about a deeper connection still lingered.

"That was awesome!" Kathleen yelled a little too loudly for the interior of the truck. "Wow, sorry I'm being so loud. I think my hearing is shot."

"My hearing is shot too, but my body is still vibrating from the pulse of the music," Cassie added.

"That's just my close proximity to you," Kathleen said as she snuggled into Cassie's arms.

Jemini laughed, shifting sideways in her seat so she could see them and Steph. "I had a great time too. Thanks for suggesting it."

"It's been a long time since I've been to a bar, but I can say I've never enjoyed a club as much as I did tonight," Steph contributed.

Jemini watched Steph's hands on the steering wheel as she maneuvered the truck around a slower moving vehicle on the interstate. It would be a long time before she was able to forget those hands on her body. Now that the physical contact was over, she needed to learn more about Steph and see if they could connect with something more than anger and lust. "What do you normally do for fun?" she asked.

"Steph plays in the dirt," Cassie answered for Steph.

She looked from Cassie back to Steph, waiting for an explanation. "Dirt?"

Steph shrugged. "Since both my parents were landscapers and enjoyed planting flowers, I guess I inherited it naturally."

"Steph did all the flowerbeds around Dorothy's house," Cassie added.

"I noticed how beautiful those were the first time I went to the house. You did a great job, Steph." She touched Steph's arm, letting her hand rest lightly there for a few seconds. It was the first time she called her Steph out loud and it seemed to fit. Stephanie was the little girl she grew up with, but Steph was the woman she had become.

Steph smiled at her. "So what do you do for fun?"

"I work."

"You're an attorney, right?" Cassie asked.

Jemini nodded, bracing herself for the usual criticism that came after her profession was revealed. It wasn't really the topic she wanted to discuss at the moment. Not very many people had a high opinion of lawyers and she wasn't in the mood to justify her career tonight. Especially in front of Steph.

"How did you manage to get so much time off?" Kathleen asked.

"She's a partner," Steph said softly.

Jemini studied Steph's profile, but after a few seconds it was clear Steph wasn't going to make eye contact with her. "Did you run a check on me?"

Steph shrugged.

"Before or after I came to Riverview?"

"Does it make a difference?"

"It does to me."

Steph gave her an evil smile. "I didn't run a check on you. The dispatch report from the night your car broke down listed a contact number for the law firm of Thompson, Myers, and Rivers. I made the connection."

"That was mean, Steph," Kathleen chastised from the backseat. "A background check would have been low."

Steph glanced in the rearview mirror at Kathleen. "Do you think your retired police officer partner didn't use her connections to check out potential suitors?"

Kathleen put some space between her and Cassie. "Did you run a background check on me?"

Cassie slapped the back of Steph's head. "Let's change this conversation before more than one of us are sleeping in the doghouse tonight." She pulled Kathleen back into her arms. "I absolutely did not run a background check on you. Don't pay any attention to the troublemaker in the front seat."

Jemini enjoyed the banter between the three women and wished she felt more of a part of it. Clearly Steph and Cassie had been friends for a while and she would use the first opportunity to ask Kathleen about it. Any details she could get on the years she had been out of Steph's life would help her to understand the person Steph had become.

"Okay, new topic. Who has the funniest coming out story?" Kathleen asked.

"Coming out or being busted out?" Steph asked.

"Either."

"I'll go first then," Steph continued. "I'd just turned seventeen and I thought I knew everything. Mom and Dad had my first coed birthday party even though I really just wanted one girl there. So I took her and we snuck out to the landscaping shed about halfway through the party. I'd never kissed a girl but I knew I wanted to and she was willing. We mostly giggled our way through a make-out session only to find out Dorothy was outside the shed the whole time."

"Oh no," Cassie groaned with sympathy. "What was she doing out there?"

"She was putting air in her bicycle tire. When I thought about it later, I remembered the door to the shed was open when we arrived. I was just too excited to think about it then."

This was the moment Jemini had been waiting for. Now she would get to hear how she had managed to be so close to Dorothy and still be a lesbian. She asked softly, "What did Dorothy say?"

"I think she was shocked at first, but later we laughed about it. She told me she wouldn't rat me out to Mom and Dad, but she encouraged me to be honest with them. Best advice I ever received. When I did finally tell them, it made us closer."

What? Surely she had heard Steph wrong. *Dorothy wasn't upset? There was no condemnation or hurled insults?* She had to hear the words from Steph so she could believe them. "Dorothy was okay with you being a lesbian?" she asked.

Steph shrugged. "Well, yeah. She was cool with it."

She turned in her seat and leaned against the door. Her life was spinning upside down. As a teenager, she had been forced to choose a life of being who she was or connecting with the grandmother she longed to be with. When she had gotten old enough for her mother to explain their sudden departure from Dorothy's house, she had been shocked with the harsh words Dorothy had used to condemn Jemini's mother when Aries came out to her. When she came to terms with being a lesbian herself, Dorothy's words still haunted her. She knew she would never be loved by Dorothy again. There would never be another chance to reconnect with the grandmother she missed so much.

She barely heard Cassie, Kathleen, and Steph's voices as they continued to tell stories for the rest of the ride back to Lake View. Several times, she could feel Steph's eyes on her, but she couldn't bring herself to look over at her. She wasn't angry at Steph, but she couldn't put her feelings into words. She was ready to curl into a ball in the privacy of her own space. When they pulled in front of her cabin, she climbed out and waved good-bye. She didn't wait for Steph to get out of the truck or even look back at her. Quickly she closed the cabin door behind her and sank to the floor, leaning against the wall. The tears fell whether she wanted them to or not.

CHAPTER ELEVEN

Steph frowned as she watched Jemini close the door behind her.

"That was weird," Cassie said, looking at Kathleen.

"I agree. I'm not sure at what point we lost her, but I noticed she had gotten quiet. I was going to talk with her when we got back. I didn't expect her to run inside so quickly."

"I think talking to her would be a good idea. Steph, do you want to come over to the house? We can have a drink," Cassie suggested.

"No, I have a case I should go check out. Footprints outside a woman's window. Might be nothing, but I'd like to catch someone and ease her mind."

"Okay," Cassie hesitated. "Would you like some company?"

Steph shrugged. "Sure. It's probably going to be boring though. Just sitting outside her house watching."

"Sounds like fun. That okay with you?" Cassie asked Kathleen.

"Go, ahead. I'm just going to bed. Please be careful, though. Both of you."

Cassie climbed back into the truck, and they waited for Kathleen to enter the house before leaving.

"What do you think was wrong with Jemini?" Cassie asked.

"I don't know. I thought we had a great time tonight. She even said as much when we left the bar."

"Maybe it was the talk about the background check."

"I guess."

"Maybe she has something horrible in her past that she doesn't want you to find out about," Cassie joked.

She knew Cassie was only trying to lighten the mood, but it bothered her that she might have done something to upset Jemini.

After a few seconds, Cassie changed topics. "So tell me where we're going."

"Do you know Sondra Pace? She lives on Wymer Street."

"I don't think so."

"Well, she lives alone and her garage was broken into a while back. Then a couple nights ago she discovered footprints outside her windows."

"Hmmm...disgruntled stalker boyfriend?" Cassie asked.

"That was my first thought too, but she claims not. I'm hoping it's a teenager enjoying a peep show."

"Just one set of footprints?"

"Yep."

"And no one else has reported the same problem?"

"Correct, but she's the only single woman on her block."

"What did they steal from the garage?"

"She couldn't identify anything specifically. I don't think she spent much time in it. She said most of the tools were left by the previous owner. Her dad had tinkered in there when she first moved in, but he passed away two years ago."

She pulled to a stop across the street from Sondra's house and called in her location to the police dispatch. There were minimal lights on in each house, and the streetlights created stationary streams of yellow along the sidewalks. Sondra's house, like most of the others, was a brick rancher on less than an acre of property. The area between and behind the houses on both sides of the street was filled with bushes and trees that had developed over the years since the houses had been built. The occasional decorative tree created dark spots along the road, and Steph searched for any movement. Without Cassie she probably would have worked her way in on foot again, but she had the feeling Cassie wanted to talk and they couldn't do that on Sondra's back porch.

"We should move closer on foot," Cassie suggested.

Steph glanced at her. "I thought you wanted to talk."

Cassie shrugged. "Talking is overrated. I think you like her and it's clear she likes you. Now you just have to figure out how hard you want to work at making it something more permanent."

"You make it sound so simple."

"Not at all. You need to tell her why you're so angry, and then you need to find out what happened tonight. Neither of those things will be simple or easy."

Steph rubbed her face. She respected Cassie more than anyone else in her life. They had tried dating when they first met but had quickly discovered they were better friends. She had been in a bad place in her life and wasn't willing to be out in the community. She didn't really lie, but being in a relationship put too much pressure on her at the time. She was still fairly new to the sheriff's department and feeling the stress of being a newbie. As a friend, Cassie had taught her to be herself around everyone, even her coworkers.

Cassie continued, "For tonight, though, surveillance is easy. Let's move closer."

"Take the right side and I'll circle the left. Stay in the tree line and away from the house."

"Got it," Cassie agreed.

Steph reached up and switched off the interior light before they opened their doors. After they gently closed them, they headed off in the opposite directions. She watched Cassie until she faded into the shadows, then she crossed into the wooded area between houses. Cassie had changed a lot when she met Kathleen. Changed for the good. She had always liked her quiet, gentle demeanor, but Kathleen had brought out a more relaxed personality. It was clear Cassie felt complete now. She was glad it had worked out with Kathleen. She liked both women and they seemed to fit well together.

Keeping in the shadows, she watched the backside of Sondra's house. The streetlights in the front of the house cast large shadows on the rear windows. Movement between the bushes and the house caught her attention. She strained her eyes to catch a glimpse of Cassie. Had she had time to get around the house? But why would she be so close when they had agreed to remain in the tree line? She squatted, resting one knee on the ground, hoping to avoid casting a Steph-shaped shadow across the backyard. The movement had stopped and she pulled out her phone, sending a text to Cassie.

Location?

Tree line right side. That u at the house? Cassie responded.

Nope.

Sweet. Let's box him in.

With u.

As she moved closer, she could see the suspect wore blue jeans and a dark hoodie. His arms worked up and down as he wiggled his screwdriver into the window frame.

"Stop," she commanded. "Sheriff's department. Drop the screwdriver and put your hands on the wall."

He glanced at her in surprise but did as he was told. She moved in and patted him down, tossing the wallet from his back pocket to Cassie. "Check his age."

Steph slid his cell phone into her pocket and when she didn't find any weapons or other items on his body, she wrapped a set of flex cuffs around his wrists. She contacted dispatch on her cell phone and advised that the suspect was in custody, requesting a cruiser for transport. She tucked her phone back in her pocket and pulled him off the wall. As they came around the house and into the glow of the streetlight, Cassie joined them. Her flashlight pointed at the driver's license in her hand.

"Thomas John McAllister, Jr. turned sixteen last month."

Before she could respond the porch light came on and Sondra stepped onto the porch. "I heard a noise and called nine one one. They said you were out here." She took a step closer to the edge of the porch. "Is that my burglar? I think I know him."

She pulled Junior into the light from the porch. "How do you know him?"

"I work with his father. Tom McAllister."

Steph turned as a cruiser pulled up on the street. She opened the rear door and pushed Junior inside. She leaned in and read him his rights before turning him over to her fellow deputy.

"I'm going to visit his parents first and then I'll come question him," she advised.

The deputy nodded and pulled away from the curb with Junior sitting silently in the backseat. She turned to Sondra. "Can you flip on the lights in your backyard? I want to see how much damage he did to the window."

She grabbed an evidence bag and camera from her truck and joined Cassie as they walked back around the house.

"I wonder why he targeted her," Cassie stated.

She knew Cassie's detective mind was in full operational mode and that her statement was only that and not a question. "Me too. That's why I want to visit his parents before I talk to him. Maybe his dad said something at home that piqued Junior's interest."

"At least he didn't make it through the window."

"Yeah, I'm glad we were here too."

Steph studied the window for any permanent damage and then snapped a couple of pictures. Using the edges of the evidence bag, she picked up the screwdriver and sealed it inside. Sondra had stepped onto the back porch to watch them and she looked at her. "Do you have any idea why he would be targeting you?"

"I can't think of any reason. I only met him once. He came and helped his dad move into a new office about a month ago.

He seemed quiet and was very respectful." Sondra shivered. "What was he going to do if he got in?"

"Probably just looking for money or things he could sell," she suggested, though she had trouble believing that herself. Assuming he was the same person who broke into the garage, why didn't he take anything to sell from there? "The window is fine out here. Just a few screwdriver scrapes. Do you need us to check anything inside the house?"

"No, it's all still good. I checked the piece of wood after I called nine one one." As if noticing for the first time that Steph was in civilian clothes, she grimaced. "Thanks for coming out on your night off and for catching him."

"No problem. This is my friend, Cassie Thomas."

Sondra gave Cassie a nod. "Thanks for helping out."

"My pleasure. I'm really glad we caught him."

"Go back to bed, Ms. Pace, and I'll give you an update when I know something," Steph offered.

"Could you do it before work on Monday? I don't want to face Tom without knowing more."

"I understand."

"Thanks again," she said as she closed the door.

Steph and Cassie walked back to the truck as the light from the porch went dark. "I should probably drop you off before I go wake up Junior's parents."

"Yeah. They aren't going to be happy to see you and having a civilian hanging around would probably make things worse. Thanks for letting me play, though."

"As I told you before, when resort life gets boring, sign on as a reserve deputy and I'll let you play more often."

Cassie laughed. "Yeah, Kathleen would love that."

* * *

Steph dropped Cassie off and woke up the McAllisters. Tom and Margaret didn't have much to say about their son's trespassing. At first they were surprised, but then they admitted John hadn't been acting right lately. She asked them to accompany her to the station so she could question him. She assured them unless anything more came out John would be arraigned when Judge Starkey arrived in his office at nine the next morning.

At the station, Steph allowed the parents to meet with their son alone first. She watched through the two-way glass as they each hugged him. "Did he say anything on the drive over?" she asked the deputy beside her.

Deputy Brian Harris was a few inches shorter than her with coal-black hair. Though he looked scrawny at first glance, his legs and arms were muscular, and he didn't shy away from physical confrontations if they were needed. He was one of the newest deputies in the department and always ended up on the late night shift. Which meant he worked the bar closings and other hubs of drunken activity that brought out the worst in people.

"I tried to engage him, but he remained silent. You might not get anything out of him."

"I'm counting on mommy and daddy to help in that area. Any ideas on why he might have targeted Sondra Pace?"

"I got nothing. I don't even think I've seen her out at any of the bars."

"He's only sixteen anyway."

"Really? Okay. Could it be gang-related then?"

She raised her eyebrows. "An initiation? Maybe. And he chose her house because he knew there wasn't a husband to chase him." She was silent for a second while she thought about this option. She didn't like to think that this might be possible, but they had seen a few signs of gang graffiti on an empty warehouse lately so maybe a group had moved up from Pensacola. "So, what was he planning to do when he got inside?"

Brian shook his head. "That's the mystery. Maybe he would have taken something to prove he'd been inside. You should talk to Jared since the kid is so young."

"He's still working with the high school kids?"

"Yep."

She nodded. Deputy Jared Miller would be on duty at seven, and she would probably be able to catch up with him before she headed home. She pulled open the door to the interrogation room and took a seat across from Junior and his parents.

"You go by John, right?" she asked.

He nodded.

"Okay, John. I'm sure the officer told you when he brought you in here that this room is under video surveillance." Steph waited for him to nod again. She needed him to begin speaking so she started small.

"John, I need you to state your name for the record."

"Thomas John McAllister, Junior." His voice was squeaky and he didn't look like a tough kid trying out for gang acceptance.

"You understand why you were arrested, right?"

He nodded again.

"Can you tell me why you were at the Pace residence tonight?"

He stared at his lap until his father nudged his shoulder. "Speak, son."

"I didn't know it was her house."

"Okay," Steph said. "Whose house did you think it was?"

"A friend."

"Does your friend have a name?"

"Troy."

Of course, the next logical question would be asking if he entered all of his friends' houses with a screwdriver, but she knew that would only put him on the defensive. So she held her sarcasm instead jotting down what he said on her notepad. She wrote slowly to stall for time. He was developing a short answer rhythm, and she didn't want this to be a question-and-answer session so she changed tactics.

"John, what time did you leave your parents' house tonight?"

He glanced back and forth between his parents. "Ten thirty."

His parents had already told her they didn't know John was even out of the house. He had gone to his bedroom at the normal time, and they had told him goodnight around ten when they went to bed.

"Tell me everything that happened when you left your parents' house tonight."

She jotted down a few more notes and then stared at John. His focus was again on his lap. She took a sip of her coffee and then set it gently on the table. She gave his parents a nod of warning and then slammed her hand on the table in front of John. His head whipped up.

"Now, John. I'd like to go to bed before dawn and I'm sure your parents would too."

He swallowed hard. "I met some friends at the convenience store."

She made a note. It would be easy to check the video surveillance to confirm that information and get the identities of his friends. No need to push him to rat them out. She made a motion for him to continue.

"They said there was a party, but we couldn't enter from the front door. We had to come in through the window in the back so the neighbors wouldn't see."

John's mother shook her head, and Steph lifted a hand for her to remain silent. She made the motion for him to continue again.

"That's it. You caught me trying to get into the party."

Steph took another sip of her coffee as she stared at him. His thin face looked almost gaunt and his eyes were red and bloodshot. His gaze traveled around the room never staying on one spot longer than a few seconds. She didn't need to tell him his story was lame. His inability to look her in the eye told her that he knew this tale wasn't going to hold up.

"Let's see if I got this right. Your friends told you to break into a house because there was a party going on inside." She slapped the table again, making John look at her. "So, why were you alone? Where were your friends?"

"I was supposed to call them when I got inside."

She closed her eyes for a second, looking down at her notepad. Those were the first words she believed, and it made her cringe to think John and his friends would have been inside Sondra's house.

"How did you get to Wymer Street?"

"I walked."

"John, I'm going to step outside with your parents and I need you to think about the story you just told us. And it was a story. There's no one in this room who believes the tale you just told. When I come back in I want the real story."

She didn't wait for him to acknowledge that he understood. His chin was already resting against his chest anyway with his eyes focused on his lap. She motioned his parents to follow her. She took them into the viewing room next door and stared at John through the glass. He still had his hands on his lap, but his forehead now rested on the table. She turned and leaned against the glass, leaving his parents with a view of their son.

"What do you guys think of his story?"

Tom glanced at his wife and then spoke. "It was crap."

Margaret nodded.

"How do we get him to tell us the truth?" she asked. She already had a plan but she wanted to give them a chance first.

Tom threw up his hands. "I'm not sure what to do with him. I thought we'd raised him to be honest with us, but clearly we have a problem."

Margaret touched his arm. "This might be the first time he snuck out, Tom."

"Oh, come on, Margaret, you don't believe that, do you? I bet he has been doing this for months, maybe even years."

Steph interrupted their argument. "I'm going to leave you guys to talk with him. I want to get the surveillance video from the store and see if I can identify his friends. There are several hours between when he left your house and when we caught him. I'd like to know what he was doing during that time. I'd also like to drug test him. With your permission, of course."

Margaret gasped, but Tom nodded. "Yes, I'd like to know too." He put an arm around Margaret's shoulder and patted it.

She escorted them back to the interrogation room. She enlisted help from another deputy for the drug test and asked him to monitor the McAllisters from the viewing room until she returned.

The owner of the convenience store had just arrived for dayshift when she pulled into the lot. He quickly made her a copy of the surveillance video and she returned to the sheriff's department. Jared was at his desk when she entered and she popped the DVD into his computer. He leaned back in his chair, stretching his long legs out underneath the desk. His blond hair was almost white and the wispy stubble on his chin did nothing to make him appear older. His pressed uniform had been altered to fit his thin body, making him appear even taller and thinner.

"Do you know of any gang activity at the high school?" she asked as she took a seat beside him.

He shook his head. "Nothing that I've noticed and no drug busts this year either."

"I've got a sixteen-year-old claiming he was invited to a party that required entrance through a back window with a screwdriver."

Jared laughed and then frowned. "Sorry, that's not funny. Well, it is, but not really. It certainly doesn't sound right though. Let me do some checking and see what I can come up with."

"Sounds good. Can you help me identify the other two yahoos with my guy?"

He tapped a couple of keys to start the video playing.

"Should be around ten thirty."

Jared advanced the tape and, true to his word, John showed up around ten forty-five. He was wearing blue jeans and a dark red sweatshirt. Not the shirt he had on now. He went in the store and came back out with a bottle of soda. His friends showed up around eleven and they stood around talking for almost an hour. A few minutes after midnight, the video showed headlights graze the parking lot and John and his friends walked out of camera range toward the car.

"Can you fast forward until daylight and make sure none of them came back?" Steph asked as she leaned back in her chair. "Looks like someone in a car picked them up about midnight. Can you put names to the other two faces?"

"The video isn't very clear, but I know who John McAllister hangs out with." Jared pulled a yearbook from his desk drawer and began flipping pages. "My guess, based on the crew cut, is Troy Berry and this guy is probably Alan Mickey."

They compared the yearbook photos to the video and Steph nodded her head in agreement, jotting down both names on her notepad.

He stood. "I'll see if I can track down another surveillance camera that might show the car."

"That would be great. Thanks. I'm going to talk with John again. If I don't get anywhere, I'll pick up the other two boys on Monday."

"Check with me before you leave and I should have something for you."

She returned to the interrogation room, relieving the deputy she had left watching the McAllisters. As she stepped inside, John was wiping his eyes and his parents looked grief-stricken.

She sank into the chair across from them. "John, I've been checking out your story." She glanced at her notes. "Do you think Troy and Alan will give me the same story that you did?"

He looked at her in surprise.

"Yes, we know who you were with last night and we also know you got into a car. Do you want to tell me who was driving?"

"I don't know his name."

"Okay, what can you tell me about him? Or his car."

"He was the one who told us about the party, but he wasn't from around here."

She shook her head. "At this point you haven't left me any options, John. You've lied and made up far-fetched stories. I'm going to hold you for the weekend."

Margaret started to cry.

Steph looked at her apologetically. "I'm sorry, Mrs. McAllister. I know you would like to take your son home today, but I can't release him with this story. If he wants to leave today, he needs to come clean with the truth."

Jared stuck his head inside the room and motioned for Steph to follow him. She stepped into the hallway and closed the door behind her.

"There aren't any surveillance cameras that cover the convenience store parking lot, but Jo had a camera that catches the road. Not much traffic at that hour, so I'm sure it was a light blue sedan and I was able to grab a partial plate number. I'm running it now." He motioned at the room behind her. "Get anything from him?"

"Nothing." She rubbed her face. She was beyond tired. There wasn't really any reason not to put John in Juvenile Detention. He had been uncooperative and really didn't deserve her support or a break of any kind. "I'm thinking about putting him in juvi for the rest of the weekend."

"I hate to see it come to that, but you've spent hours with him and he's giving you nothing." Jared looked around. "We could keep him here. We have at least one empty cell."

"I'd consider that if we use the rubber room. I really don't want anything to happen to him. That's why I'm a little afraid of putting him in juvi. I just can't figure out what's going on with him."

"Book him and I'll go check out the room."

She watched Jared walk away. Her head was too foggy to continue questioning John. She could always come back in later today or on Sunday if his parents were willing. She stepped back inside the room.

"Last chance, John. We have the car and it's just a matter of time until we get the owner. Do you want to tell me what really happened last night?"

He hesitated, and she thought for a second he was going to come clean, but then he shook his head.

"Okay, stand up. Let's go get you booked in for the weekend." She glanced at his parents. "If you would like to see him again before you leave, I can come get you when he gets settled."

Margaret's head was buried in her hands as she sobbed, but Tom nodded.

"It'll take about twenty minutes, but I'll come get you."

She took John's arm and escorted him from the room. While she fingerprinted and photographed him, she continued to talk. She worked on his feelings for his mother, talking about how torn up she was about what he was doing to her. He didn't offer any more answers, but at one point she could see glistening in the corner of his eye. She hoped she was right about him and that he deserved her benefit of the doubt. It wouldn't be the first time she was played by a kid, but she couldn't stop believing there was good in them.

As she locked the door to John's cell, leaving him only a mattress to lay on, she took one last opportunity to play on his emotions. "John, we've been up for over thirty hours now and we're all exhausted. Get some sleep, but when you wake up, work through all of this. It doesn't have to end like this. I have no doubt that you love your parents and that you don't want to put them through any of this. If you want my help, you have to tell me the truth."

He sank onto the mattress and held his head in his hands. "You don't understand," he mumbled.

"I'll understand if you tell me."

He shook his head. "I want to see my parents."

She nodded at the deputy watching the cells and returned to the interrogation room. She placed a cup of coffee in front of John's parents and took a sip of her own before speaking. "I think he's too scared of his friends to tell the truth."

His parents nodded.

"I could try to make him more scared of the police and what his future could hold, but honestly I don't like to do that to kids. I'd rather he make the decision on the right thing to do than to make him even more scared. So, when you talk to him just keep pushing him to be honest. If he tells the whole story, then we can counter whatever has him frightened. I told the deputy to give you thirty minutes, but you won't be able to see him again until Monday. He can call collect, though, so if he wants to talk to me, just let the desk sergeant know and I'll come in." She stood. "Go through the doors at the rear of the station and follow the hallway. The deputy will meet you there."

She made a quick stop at Jared's desk before heading out. He was still trying to track the license plate and didn't have any news for her. She asked him to call if something came through, then climbed into her truck and made the drive back to her house. She waved to Agnes, sitting on the front porch but didn't have the energy to stop and talk. She only wanted to fall into bed, but her clothes were ready to stand on their own and she knew she had to shower. With her eyes already closed, she went through the motions of washing her hair and body before falling onto her bed naked.

CHAPTER TWELVE

Jemini's head ached and her eyes were scratchy. She was relieved that the tears had finally ran out by daybreak. Knowing now that Steph had gotten to live with the love and acceptance that she had longed for hurt far deeper than she could put into words.

She lay in bed long after she had awakened from her couple-hour nap, struggling to make sense of the story her mother had told her. Unfortunately she had already married Jemini's father when she came to terms with her desire to be with another woman. Though she held on for Jemini's sake, she knew she would have to leave eventually. She never cheated on Jake and it helped that he was away so much of the time. She had been on the verge of breaking the news to him when he was killed. Taking care of Jemini on her waitress salary would have been a struggle and she was relieved when Dorothy offered to let them stay with her permanently.

Everything had been wonderful until Jemini's mother revealed her deepest secret to the woman she had thought of as a second mother. Dorothy's reaction had been shocking and disapproving, leaving her no choice but to take her daughter and run. Tears threatened Jemini's eyes again and she wiped them with the sheet covering her before pushing it away. Today she would quickly finish looking at the items Dorothy had left behind, and then tomorrow she would return home, leaving this nightmare in the past forever. She brushed away the lingering thoughts of Steph and their shared kiss. No matter what she longed for, she knew she couldn't spend time with Steph without thinking of how Steph had gained the grandmother she had lost. The grandmother Jemini had ached to return to but didn't, believing she would face the same harsh condemnation her mother had lived with until her dying day.

After showering and trying to pull herself together, she finally left the cabin. Her thoughts were focused on completing her agenda in Riverview and returning home. She didn't notice Kathleen heading up the walk toward her until she spoke.

"Good morning, Jemini."

She stopped at the door of her car and turned. "Good morning." She glanced at her watch. She wasn't trying to be rude, but she did want Kathleen to realize she had somewhere to be.

"Do you have time for a walk?"

She wanted to say no. Really badly, she wanted to say no. Her emotions were frayed, and she knew Kathleen would pull at the loose strings. She also feared Kathleen's gentle approach would unravel her further.

"Sure," she said, surprising herself at her willingness to subject her fragile emotional state to Kathleen's intuitiveness. The truth was she needed Kathleen's logical mind and words to help make sense of everything she was feeling. She easily fell into step with Kathleen as they headed for the path along the lake.

Kathleen reached down to pet two dogs as they approached at a run. They were both black with curly fur and a white spot on their chests. "Meet Zoey and Pandy," she said to Jemini.

Jemini offered her hand to both girls before giving them each a pet. They stood patiently until the petting stopped and then they ran ahead, splashing at the edge of the lake. "I'd noticed them hanging nearby at the cookout last night. They're your dogs?"

"Yes, Cassie got them both as puppies, but they've happily welcomed me into the family."

"Dogs are great like that. I've often thought about getting a pet, but my hours at work are long. It wouldn't be fair to anything but maybe a goldfish."

Kathleen chuckled. "No, I guess they don't look for human companionship very often."

Jemini looked around the lake as they reached the back side of it. Unlike on previous days the beach was empty and quiet. The water looked cool and inviting, barely stirred by the fountain in the middle. She wondered what it would be like to live here or at least nearby.

"You seemed upset when we dropped you off last night," Kathleen stated.

Jemini braced herself. She could feel the unraveling begin. She knew Kathleen's eyes were on her, but she was relieved when she didn't push further. Kathleen hadn't lived in Riverview for her whole life like Steph or even for years like Cassie, but Kathleen could still have insight that she herself couldn't see.

"Did you tell me that you had met Dorothy?"

"I did. She was working on the Riverview Christmas decorations committee last year and came to the resort looking for donations."

"Was she nice? To you, I mean. Everyone knows you and Cassie are a couple, right?"

"She was nice. Of course, she was hoping we'd give her money. Is there something specific you're looking for? Cassie might be able to help you, but Steph would be the best source of information."

"I've thought of that, but it's not really something I can talk to Steph about." She wanted to, though. She wanted to understand why Dorothy had changed her mind. To understand why she had to live her life alone. She chose her words carefully. "I discovered something unsettling last night."

"Something about Dorothy?"

"Kind of." She took a deep breath. "Dorothy kicked my mother out for being a lesbian."

"Wow," Kathleen said, surprise showing on her face. "Does Steph know that?"

"I don't really know what Steph knows, because we haven't talked about it."

"So, last night's discovery was finding out that Dorothy knew about Steph being a lesbian?"

"Yes. I needed—still need—time to process all that."

"I certainly understand that, but I'm here if you want help."

Jemini nodded. If she was to have this conversation with anyone it should be with Steph. Kathleen could help her categorize her thoughts, but she didn't have the answers. "I should probably go."

"Okay. Maybe we can talk in the morning?"

She gave Kathleen a wave as she climbed into her car. She did enjoy her walks and talks with her. Her job kept her from having friends or even the time to hang out with friends. She could see herself spending time with Cassie and Kathleen. Unfortunately, Steph's face kept appearing in the picture too. She had enjoyed their time together so much last night. It was hard for her to imagine going back to Chattanooga to be alone. Today she couldn't even find any enthusiasm for her job, which had been the one thing that had sustained her through the years.

Dorothy's house was quiet when she arrived. She could see Steph's truck parked beside her house, but she resisted the urge to knock on her door, focusing again on her agenda to clear things up and get home. She unlocked the door and was preparing to go in when she heard the sound of a vehicle approaching.

Richard Greene stepped out of his car with his briefcase and began talking before he made it to the porch.

"Ms. Rivers, are you ready to sign the paperwork today? The developer is pushing for a fast closing and would like to reach an agreement." He stepped up on the porch beside her. "I have the paperwork all ready."

"I'm not ready to sign yet," she said, more harshly than she intended. She dropped her head, shocked by her own words. Why wasn't she ready to sign? She had decided to finish up quickly and return home; selling the house would be the quickest option. She looked up again to see Brandon standing at the corner of the house, and she shook her head at Richard. "No. I'll call you on Monday and we can talk about the options. I'm not going to be rushed into anything."

Richard, to her surprise, returned to his car without another word.

She sat down on the steps and watched Brandon. He hung at the edge of the house, kicking dirt with the toe of his shoe.

"Do you want to sit, Brandon?"

He walked toward her, scuffing his feet.

"Did you hear what Richard said?"

He nodded, sitting down beside her. "Who is the developer? And why does he want to buy our house?"

She smiled. She wanted to put her arm around him and pull him close, telling him everything would be okay. How could she tell him that, though? She was going to sell his house.

The idea hit her fast and hard. As a partner in one of Chattanooga's top law firms, she was set financially. Money was not an issue. So, why sell the house? She could just give it away. Give it to Steph. Placing her arm around Brandon, she gave him a squeeze.

"A developer is someone who buys land and then builds something on it."

"But our house is already here."

"That's right, and I'm not going to sell it to him. In fact, I might not sell it at all."

He looked up at her. "Would you live here with us?"

She smiled. "No, but someone else will probably move in. Would that be okay with you?"

"Maybe another kid like me."

"Ms. Agnes would probably rather have someone closer to her age, but maybe she would have grandkids."

"Ms. Dorothy was a grandmother, but no kids ever visited her. She said I was her favorite kid. She made me cookies and always had Teenage Mutant Ninja Turtle Band-Aids."

"No Barbie or princess stuff for you, eh?"

"No way. Ms. Dorothy said I was the man of the house and I should stick to reptiles over princesses." He scuffed his shoe on the step. "I don't like snakes though."

"I never liked them either, but turtles and lizards are cool."

His eyes grew large. "You like lizards?"

"Well, I did when I was your age. I would capture one and play with it all day until my grandmother would make me set it free."

"Wow," Brandon said, clearly impressed with this knowledge. "If you lived here, I could bring you a lizard every day."

She laughed and shook her head. "Let's not get crazy."

He stood. "I'm going to see if I can find one now. I hope you like the green ones. They're the easiest to find."

"Brandon, please no," Jemini called to his disappearing back.

She stood with a glance in the direction Brandon disappeared. She hoped he wouldn't be able to find any lizards today. She stopped inside the door and let her eyes adjust to the dim lighting. The box she had removed from the closet two days ago still sat on the chair where she left it. She flipped on a nearby lamp and sat down on the floor, pulling the box down with her. Opening the lid, she was surprised to see it full of letters instead of pictures. She pulled out the top one and saw it was addressed to her with "return to sender" clearly marked over the address. She rapidly sorted through the rest of the box. Each letter carried a different postmark with dates spanning over the last eighteen years. There were cards and letters, all with her name on them and her mother's block handwriting marking them "return to sender."

She played with the most recent letter, tossing it back and forth between her hands. It wasn't worn or faded like some of the others in the box, though it had a fold on one corner. Like the page of a paperback novel, that someone intended to return to. She slid her thumb under the corner of the flap and pried it open, letting the folded page fall out.

Even though the letter was addressed to her, she felt like she was reading someone else's diary. Each time she reached the bottom of the page, her eyes returned to the beginning again as the words began to sink into her soul. Dorothy's remorse at the continued absence of Jemini in her life immediately brought tears to her eyes. After reading several letters, she skipped to the oldest in the box. Dorothy started with apologies for not trying to stop Jemini's mother from leaving and for letting time pass before attempting to contact them. The letters referenced others written to Jemini's mother although she didn't see them in the box and a quick check of the closet produced no additional boxes. She wondered if maybe her mother had kept the letters Dorothy wrote to her instead of returning them as she had done with the ones addressed to Jemini.

As the sun faded, the shadows crept across the floor toward her, but she didn't move. She opened letter after letter, reading the words she had longed to hear from her grandmother. Words filled with unconditional love and acceptance for her mother and for the woman Jemini had become. When she finally read the last one, she closed the lid on the box and hugged her legs to her body. Resting her head on her knees, she cried. Deep sobs racked her body as she thought about all the years Dorothy had invited her to visit. Her grandmother had lived with the guilt of the words she had spoken to Jemini's mother. Words she tried to take back and apologies Jemini was never given the opportunity to accept.

* * *

Steph stepped out of her house and squinted at the setting sun. The nap she had taken wasn't enough to make her feel whole again, but as soon as she noticed Jemini's car in the driveway she couldn't go back to sleep. The job had kept her mind occupied since they had returned from the bar, but now she needed to talk with her. She showered and dressed quickly, crossing to the front porch. Brandon met her on the stairs, and she almost gave a squeal when he pushed a small green lizard toward her face.

"Isn't it cool? I caught it for Ms. Jemini."

Steph raised her eyebrows. "Is she expecting it?"

"Oh, yes. We talked earlier and she told me how much she liked them."

She put her arm around him, holding the hand with the lizard away from her. She knocked on the door and was preparing to knock a second time when Jemini finally opened the door. She took a step back, pulling Brandon with her. Jemini's face was red and splotchy. It was clear she had been crying. She wanted to pull her into her arms. "What's wrong?"

"Everything's fine," Jemini said as she knelt in front of Brandon. "Let's see what you got."

Brandon eagerly stepped forward, holding the kicking lizard up for her to see. "I found him behind the house."

"He's very cute."

"Cute? You've got to be kidding me," Steph said, shaking her head and offering her hand to help Jemini to her feet.

"Thanks for showing him to me. Can you return him to his home now?" Jemini asked.

"And then check in with your mom. It's almost dinnertime," Steph suggested.

"Okay," Brandon said disappointedly.

Steph gave his shoulder a pat. "It was a good catch, buddy. Be proud."

He gave her a smile and jumped off the porch, disappearing around the side of the house.

"Did you really ask him to catch that for you?" she asked as she stepped in the house, closing the door behind them.

Jemini smiled. "Not really, but it was sweet."

She leaned against the couch and stared at Jemini. She could see that her face was puffy and tear-streaked and her eyes were red. "Want to tell me what's wrong now?"

Jemini shook her head, brushing a hand toward the box on the floor. "I found some letters from Dorothy."

"Letters to who?"

"Me."

Steph frowned. "Addressed to you and never mailed?"

"No, addressed to me and marked 'return to sender.'"

"You never received them?"

"No, Mom must have refused them."

Steph sat down on the floor and opened the box. "Do you mind?"

Jemini shrugged and sat down beside her, handing her the most recent letter.

* * *

The letter she handed Steph didn't address the reason her mother had taken her and left. She was glad about that. This wasn't the way she wanted Steph to hear the details. In fact, she wasn't sure she ever wanted her to know. Steph would never be able to understand the rejection she felt from Dorothy. Especially since Dorothy had so readily accepted Steph. She watched her face as she read the letter. Then she slowly folded it and placed it back in the envelope before handing it back to Jemini.

"She waited every year for you to arrive. Like she expected it." Steph shook her head. "But all along she knew you hadn't received the letter. It doesn't make sense."

"She waited for me to arrive?"

"Not just waited. She would bake all week. More cookies and pies than any of us could eat and then on Saturday, Agnes and I would sit with her on the porch. They would talk and reminisce while Dorothy watched the driveway." Steph shook her head again. "Why would she think you were coming if the letter was returned to her?"

Jemini stood and began to pace. "In some spots she referenced letters she had written to my mother. I didn't find any of them here. Maybe she made the same invitation to her and since those letters weren't returned to her—"

"She thought your mother might bring you."

"Mom never mentioned any letters to me. She never mentioned Dorothy again after the day we left except when she finally explained to me why we had to leave and couldn't go back. The letters addressed to me all went to Mom's house. When she died last year, I had her mail forwarded to my house, but that only lasts for six months." Jemini reached the wall separating the two rooms and turned back to Steph. "Based on the date of each envelope, I don't think she had written the letter for this year yet. She didn't know Mom was dead."

She felt her eyes fill with tears again. She didn't think her body had anything left to give, but the sympathy and compassion she saw on Steph's face took her breath away. In only a second all the years of pain faded and she felt the love Steph had grown up with. Everything she had missed came crashing down on her, leaving her overwhelmed with emotion. She rubbed her face and began to pace again. Would she ever be able to completely confide in Steph? Could there be anything between them if she couldn't?

* * *

Steph stood and followed Jemini as she paced into the kitchen. She had seen the tears start to fall before Jemini turned. She wished she knew how to ease her pain, but the truth was she didn't know what was causing it. Surely she wasn't mourning Dorothy's death. Jemini could have come back anytime over the years and she chose not to.

Jemini turned and started back toward her, her beauty overcoming the resentment and confusion Steph had been feeling. Her dark hair was thick and curly, falling around her face and giving her a hidden, mysterious appearance that appealed to Steph's detective side. She couldn't turn away from her or even pull her eyes away. Everything about Jemini fascinated her. She wanted to be closer to her. She wanted to hold her and comfort her, but she also wanted to feel her and taste her. She didn't want to watch her leave when all of this was over. She wanted Jemini to want to stay and to make Riverview her home.

The candy from Jemini's sugar overload days before still lay on the kitchen counter. Steph spotted the bright red sour balls, and her mouth watered, remembering the taste of Jemini's mouth mixed with the tangy sweetness. Without thinking, she crossed to the counter and popped several balls into her mouth. She turned and met Jemini as she circled the counter, still pacing.

She bit into the hard candy shell, her eyes squinting at the sour explosion that filled her mouth. She pulled Jemini into her arms and pressed her mouth to hers. Sliding her tongue across her lips, she shared the essence of the tart candy. Jemini's response was immediate; she opened her mouth, allowing Steph to push what was left of the fast-dissolving balls of sugar into her mouth. The candy was quickly forgotten as their kiss deepened. Steph's hands found flesh between Jemini's T-shirt and shorts, and she took advantage of the opportunity. Running her hands up Jemini's sides, she pushed her thumbs across the hard peaks of her nipples.

Jemini took a step back, her eyes hazy with desire. "You make me forget everything I want to say."

"What do you want to say?" Steph asked, swallowing hard.

"I've changed my mind. I'm not going to sell the house."

"What? You're not going to sell. What changed your mind? Was it my kiss?" She danced in a circle. "Oh, you're going to love it here."

Jemini frowned and then shook her head. "I'm not going to move here."

Steph's world collapsed around her. For one second, she had celebrated and had felt like her heart would burst. Everything she had ever wanted had just been given to her and she almost screamed in joy. And then Jemini had pulled the rug out from under her. Just like she had done to Dorothy for all those years. She had been stupid to think for even one second that Jemini would give her what she wanted.

* * *

The look of disappointment on Steph's face shocked Jemini, and she dropped into a nearby chair. She had been caught up in Steph's excitement, thinking that they had been celebrating the same thing. She thought she would be happy with her decision.

Steph spoke, her voice devoid of emotion. "That's great, Jemini. Everyone will be happy."

"I'm sorry if you misunderstood me. I have a home and a job in Chattanooga."

"Right. I understand."

She couldn't take the emotionless look on Steph's face. She didn't understand why Steph was closing herself off now. Their kiss had rocked her to her knees. She had given everything she had and hoped that Steph had been able to read it. She wanted more and she wanted it from Steph.

And now she was acting like there was nothing between them. That the only way there could be was if she moved to Riverview. She was willing to consider that, but not the way Steph was forcing her hand. She needed time to explore what was happening between them, but she wouldn't be pressured into making a decision that would change her whole life. She exploded from her chair. "What the hell do you want from me?"

"I want my friend back," Steph said vehemently as she turned and bolted out the front door.

She couldn't let Steph leave like this. Not with things hanging between them. She followed her to the door as Steph's phone began to ring. She heard Steph answer and respond that she was on her way. It sounded urgent and as much as she wanted to, she knew she couldn't delay her. She walked back into the house and collapsed onto the couch, Steph's words still echoing in her head.

"I want my friend back."

This time she knew Steph wasn't talking about Dorothy. She was talking about her. Steph wanted her back. For them to be together again. She wanted that too. The connection between them had been strong when they were young, but it felt even stronger now. She couldn't help but wonder how close they would be today if they hadn't been separated years ago. She was sure of one thing. Steph was right. She wanted her friend back, too, but unfortunately it wasn't that easy. She couldn't just walk away from everything she had worked for in Chattanooga. Could she?

CHAPTER THIRTEEN

Steph didn't have time to return to the sheriff's department to pick up a cruiser. She drove straight to Wymer Street and parked several houses down from Sondra's. The dispatcher had relayed a panicked call from Sondra Pace. There was someone outside her house again. She asked dispatch to send the deputies on duty for backup. She didn't wait to find out who was coming or when they would be there. If the intruder left, she would be back to working with nothing again, and she didn't want to wait days or weeks to get this guy. She wanted him tonight.

The dome light was still turned off from her visit the previous night, so Steph softly opened the door and slid out. She closed her door, resting it against the frame before gently clicking it closed. She watched the front of Sondra's house as she approached. Confident he was behind the house, she moved slowly to avoid missing anything obvious. Staying in the tree line, she moved around the house until she could see the backyard.

She watched a dark figure lift the window and heft himself onto the windowsill. He or she didn't look much taller than Steph, and the dark jeans hung off their thin body. She wanted to see what would happen if he got inside, but she couldn't risk Sondra's safety to do it. She approached quickly and pinned the intruder's lower body with her chest.

"What?" a masculine voice exclaimed as he began to kick, trying to swivel around to see who held him.

"Sheriff's department. Put your hands behind your back. Now."

Surprisingly, he did as she asked, and she fastened a flex cuff around his wrists. She lifted his feet and pushed him through the window, climbing in behind him.

"Ms. Pace, it's Deputy Williams," she called loudly. She repeated her words until she got a response from Sondra. "Don't turn on any lights."

Stepping into the hallway, she waited until Sondra followed her voice, and then she guided her to a nearby chair.

"I'm so sorry to scare you like this, but we need to find out what's going on here."

"I'm okay. I was watching the street when you arrived."

She patted Sondra's arm. "Everything's okay. Just stay right here." She pulled her cell phone from her pocket and dialed dispatch. Then she sent a text to both deputies on duty.

Got one. Stay hidden. Going to see what else we can flush out.

She received two immediate positive responses. Pulling the intruder to his feet, she patted him down, removing his cell phone from his pocket. She was relieved he wasn't carrying any kind of weapon. She guided him into the living room and pushed him back to the floor. She attached another set of flex cuffs to his feet before pulling the ski mask from his head. She recognized Troy Berry from his yearbook picture.

"All right, Troy. Want to tell me what's going on here?"

He glanced around, pretending to be surprised. "'Posed to be a party."

"Really? Skip the stupid lie and go right to the truth."

"Really. That's what I was told."

"So, after your friend John was arrested yesterday, you were still stupid enough to believe the same story."

He nodded.

Steph pulled his cell phone from her pocket and began searching his contacts. When she found Alan Mickey's number, she hit call, holding the phone to Troy's ear.

"Tell your friend you're in."

"I'm...I'm in," Troy said into the phone.

She pulled the phone away from him and ended the call before he could say more.

"Ms. Pace, please go into your bedroom and lock the door until I tell you to come out."

Sondra hurried down the hall, and Steph heard the lock click into place. She took a seat in the hallway where she could watch Troy and see the window his friend would come through. She should have been thinking about what these boys could be looking for, she knew, but her mind kept slipping back to Jemini and the look on her face when Steph had left. The hazy eyes filled with desire, which had quickly changed to anger. Jemini had succeeded in finding a way to make almost everyone happy. The news that she wouldn't sell the house was good for Agnes and Kim, but Steph knew she could never be happy without Jemini in her life.

A rustle outside the window caught her attention, drawing her focus back to the window and the entrance of a second intruder. She shook her head. This was getting crazy. She grabbed his shoulders and pulled him through the window. Placing a knee in his back, she pulled his arms behind him and bound them with a set of flex cuffs. She helped him to his feet and patted him down. Setting him on the floor beside his accomplice, she cuffed his legs too.

She sent a text to the deputies.

Got a second one. See any more out there?
Nope.
Yep. Got one in a car.

She thought for a minute before texting back.

Watch him. Don't let him leave.

She dropped to one knee in front of both boys. "Welcome to the party, Alan."

Alan's face was flushed, and he looked on the verge of tears. He was definitely her weakest link.

"Troy didn't give you up. We saw you on the surveillance cameras after we picked John up last night. Tell me what you were told to do once you got into the house."

"I…I can't. He'll kill my parents."

She frowned. "The man in the car? We have him so you and your family are safe."

Both boys looked relieved and Alan spoke first.

"There's a letter from an attorney here that we're supposed to find."

She heard Sondra gasp, and she turned to find her standing in the bedroom doorway.

Resisting the urge to lecture her about not staying locked in the bedroom, she asked, "Do you know what they're looking for?"

"Yes, but no one but my attorney knows about it. And it's locked in a safety deposit box at the bank."

Steph texted the deputies again.

Calling it off. Pick up the man in the car. Meet you out front in five.

"Who's the guy in the car?" Steph asked the boys.

They both shrugged.

"How'd you meet him?"

Alan spoke again, "He approached us at the convenience store a couple of weeks ago."

Steph stared at both of them, waiting for either to continue.

Troy picked up the story. "He offered us a hundred bucks to watch a house all night. It was easy money. We just told him if anyone came or left."

"What house?"

"Over on Digger Street. Four eighty-two, I think."

She wrote down the information and then looked at Sondra, but she shook her head.

"We did that a couple nights, and then we didn't see him for a week or so. When he came back he said the house we'd been watching was broken into and the police had our names."

"Yeah, but he could clear us if we just did another job for him," Alan added with disgust. "I didn't want to, but John figured it was easy money, and it would help clear us so we went along with it. Last night he told John his parents were in danger if he didn't get into this house."

"He didn't tell us until tonight what we were looking for," Troy finished.

She cut the ties holding their feet and helped both boys stand. She opened the front door and passed the boys to the deputy who was waiting before turning back to Sondra.

"If you don't mind, I'd like you to come down to the office and see if you can identify this guy from the car."

"Yes, definitely. I'd like to know who he is and how he knows about what I have."

"Do you mind me asking what it is?"

Sondra shook her head. "My grandfather left me a 1930s stock certificate. When I turned thirty last month, the attorney who handled his will gave it to me. I'm not sure how much it's worth, but the attorney estimated at least a hundred thousand. I brought it home with me while I decided whether to cash it or not. Last week I put it in a safety deposit box."

"And you haven't mentioned this to anyone? Not a friend or at work."

"No. No, people act weird when they know you have money. It's probably not enough to allow me to quit my job, so I didn't want to tell anyone."

"What about family members?"

"I don't have any family around here. My closest relative is a cousin in Colorado, but he's on the other side of the family. I'm the last one related to my grandfather, which is why I got the bond."

"I won't be specific in my report, so this will still be your secret. Get dressed and I'll secure the window."

Steph grabbed several boards and the hammer from the garage and secured the broken window. She waited for Sondra to back her car out of the garage, and then she led the way to the sheriff's department. Inside, she took Sondra to the viewing side of the interrogation room and allowed her to get a good look at the man from the car. She talked with one of the other deputies before joining Sondra inside the room.

"We've identified him as Charlie Ripkin. Does that name sound familiar?" Steph asked Sondra when she returned to the viewing room.

"No, but I think he might work in my attorney's office."

"Okay. We're running a check on him now." She wrote down the name of the attorney's office in Pensacola. "You're welcome to hang around or you can head back home."

"I'd like to wait until we can confirm that's where he got my information. It gives me a little closure. I really don't want any more late night visitors."

Steph led her to a small break room and fixed them both a cup of coffee. "I'll come back as soon as I know something."

* * *

Jemini took another sip of wine. Nights of no dinner and too much wine were starting to become the standard for her in Riverview. Her body involuntarily jumped at the knock on the door. If she was honest, she had been hoping Kathleen would come by. Tonight she needed a friend and she had become so comfortable around her. She pulled the door open and smiled. "Just the person I was hoping to see."

Kathleen raised her eyebrows. "Am I ranking higher than Steph?"

"For tonight at least."

"I'll take that. Can I come in or would you like to walk?"

"How about one lap and then we can return to my bottle of wine."

"I like that idea," Kathleen said. "Cassie and Chase are watching zombies, so I was very happy when I saw your car come in."

They crossed the grass to the walking path and Jemini stopped to look at the reflection of the old-fashioned streetlights on the water. "I think I might have said this before and if I didn't, I certainly thought it, but it really is beautiful here."

"It was like coming home for me the first time I came here. If you lived in Riverview, you could visit as often as you liked."

She smiled at Kathleen's not-so-subtle hint. "I've thought about staying, but the thought of starting over is a little scary."

"I understand. I felt the same way when I moved here."

"Yes, but you had Cassie to make the move easier."

"And you have Steph."

She shook her head and started walking again. "I'm not so sure about that. Seems I've managed to piss her off once again."

"Communication is not Steph's best attribute. Cassie's either, for that matter, but Cassie and I don't have the history you and Steph have. That makes it harder for you. Once everything is out in the open, I'm sure it will be easier."

"I thought I'd be making her happy since I've decided not to sell Dorothy's property."

"Wow. That's great news. So, you're going to move? You'll love it here and I'll love having you here."

"Geez. You sound just like Steph. I'm not going to live in Dorothy's house. I'm going to sign it over to Steph. I don't need or want the money, so it seemed like a good decision, but I didn't get a chance to tell her that part. She blew up when she heard I wasn't moving here."

"Well, that's great news for Agnes and Kim. What did Steph say?"

She could hear the disappointment in Kathleen's voice, and it reminded her of the disappointment on Steph's face when she told her. Why did everyone think she was going to throw away her life in Chattanooga?

Maybe the question she should be asking was why was she resisting a move to Riverview? It would be a hard commute, but she was a partner and she could make it work. She had thought about it and even mentioned it to Karen, but when faced with the assumption she was pushing back. She needed time to think all of this through before she said anything to anyone, even Kathleen.

"Jemini?"

"She said that it was great and that everyone would be happy."

"Everyone will be happy, but I'm guessing she meant everyone but her?"

Jemini shrugged. "I was trying to do the right thing."

"It's very nice of you, but I think you're missing the point."

"What point?"

"Steph wants you to stay."

She knew Steph wanted her to stay, and sometimes she wanted it too. She had certainly thought about it enough over the last few days. She wanted to tell Kathleen everything and hear someone else's logic, but words wouldn't come. Only Steph's words kept constantly echoing in her head. "*I want my friend back.*" She certainly felt the draw between them, but she wasn't sure she could let go of the past. When they reached the cabin, she held the door open for Kathleen and then followed her inside. Kathleen took a seat in the living room while she poured two glasses of wine. Sinking onto the couch across from Kathleen, Jemini took a deep breath and pulled her legs under her.

"Do you want to know the details of why my mother took me away from Dorothy?"

Kathleen nodded, taking a sip of wine.

"When my mother told Dorothy she was a lesbian, Dorothy released her wrath. She said things it took my mother years to repeat to me. My mother was in shock. She took me and ran. I always dreamed of coming back, but when I decided I liked girls better too, Mom told me what had happened. I knew then I could never come back. Dorothy wouldn't welcome me back like I'd always imagined."

Kathleen leaned forward. "And now you have to come to terms with the fact that Dorothy had accepted Steph."

"And not my mother." Her tears started to fall again. "Today I found a box of letters from Dorothy to me. Apologizing for everything and asking me to visit."

"She never mailed them?"

"She mailed them and my mother returned them."

"Oh, Jemini." Kathleen moved beside her and pulled her into her arms. "I can't imagine how painful that must be for you."

She leaned back, wiping her eyes. "I've cried more in the last week than in the last twenty years. I don't know whether to be angrier at Dorothy for not accepting my mother or my mother for sending Dorothy's apologies back or at Steph for living the life I always wanted."

"Have you told Steph all of this?"

She shook her head. "I don't know if she knows the real reason we left, but she saw the letters from Dorothy. She read one that didn't talk about the reason we left, only Dorothy's invitation for me to visit. I think now I might understand why Steph was so angry with me when I arrived. She'd watched Dorothy's disappointment every year when I didn't show up."

"But if the letters were returned why did Dorothy think you would come?"

She shrugged. "Steph and I think maybe she was sending a letter to my mother each year too. We didn't find any of those, so chances are my mom kept them and probably even read them. Which leaves me with even more questions. Why did she return only the letters addressed to me? And why didn't she tell me Dorothy was contacting her?"

"Maybe she was trying to protect you from Dorothy's criticism. I'm sure your mother was doing what she thought was best for you."

A knock sounded at the door and Jemini quickly wiped her eyes.

Kathleen patted Jemini's leg and stood. "That's probably my zombie chasers."

Chase burst through the door as soon as Kathleen opened it, but Cassie grabbed his shirt, pulling him back onto the porch. "Everything okay?" she asked.

"It will be, I think," Kathleen said with a glance at Jemini.

"Did the humans survive to fight another day?" Jemini asked Chase, who stood dancing on the porch beside Cassie.

"Oh, yes," Chase exclaimed. He immediately began to tell them everything that happened in the show they had watched.

Kathleen patted his head, letting him talk while she gave Jemini a big hug. "Chase will be right back with some leftovers from dinner. You need to eat and get a good night's sleep. Everything will be clearer in the morning, and you can talk to Steph."

She nodded. "Thanks."

Kathleen herded her family off the porch before calling over her shoulder, "I'll see you for our walk in the morning."

Jemini sat on the porch and watched the stars while she waited for Chase to return. The crickets and frogs chirping around her were comforting and she closed her eyes. So many thoughts rushed through her mind. She didn't want to be upset with her mother, but how could she not be? Her mother had made all the decisions for her. The decision to leave and the decision to never let her hear Dorothy's apologies. She would never know if her mother had responded to any of the letters and what she might have said. That upset her too.

She heard Chase's cowboy boots scuffing along the path and looked up to see him carrying a large shopping bag.

"Leenie wanted you to have a variety so she packed a lot," Chase said as he dropped the bag onto the step beside her.

"Thank you, Chase," she said, smiling at the nickname he apparently used for Kathleen.

He gave her a quick hug. "I was told to come straight back and to not disturb you."

She hugged him back and then watched him hurry in the direction of his house. She waited until he was out of sight, though she knew there were two adults on the other end waiting for his return. Two women that she had grown very fond of in just a short amount of time. She couldn't think of anyone in Chattanooga that she felt this way about. She cared about Karen, but they weren't really friends. Karen worked for her and there would always be a division between them. She would never confide in Karen the way she had with Kathleen.

The scent of garlic bread finally reached her nose, and she realized for the first time in days that she was starving. Tomorrow she would come clean with Steph and see if they could find a middle ground together. She stood, taking her bag of leftovers, and walked into the cabin.

CHAPTER FOURTEEN

Another all-nighter with too much coffee was making Steph's head feel fuzzy. She looked around the squad room at her fellow deputies. Everyone had chipped in to help her iron out the details from this crazy case, and now they were all hurrying to type out reports so they could get home.

She looked up at Jared as he approached her desk.

"Let's go get some lunch," he suggested.

All of the boys, even John, had been released to their parents. She didn't expect any charges to be brought against them, although Jared had suggested some community service to help educate them. Charlie Ripkin was in a cell and wouldn't be going anywhere for a while. Steph had filed multiple charges against him already, and the prosecutor's office was preparing more. Charlie's employer was bending over backward to convince Sondra Pace that her personal information had not been shared with anyone else. She was starving and couldn't think of a single reason not to go with Jared—except maybe that she needed sleep.

She also wanted to see Jemini. Every spare minute through the night she had thought of her beautiful face. They still had things to talk about, but she was relieved to know it wasn't Jemini's callousness that stopped her from returning at Dorothy's invitation. Though she did wonder what reasons Jemini had for not coming back, Jemini's tears had broken Steph's heart. She longed to bring back the smile she was growing so fond of.

"Lunch?" Jared nudged her.

"Sorry. I was lost in thought."

"Clearly." He laughed. "Was she beautiful?"

She ignored his question though she was afraid the heat on her face might already have confirmed his suspicions. She needed food before she could think anymore. And probably some sleep. She slowed to allow Jared to keep pace with her as they exited the sheriff's department.

"I'm driving," he said, taking the keys from her hand.

She was too tired to argue. She opened the passenger door and slid into the cruiser. The comfort of the seat pulled her into it, and she was afraid she wouldn't be able to get out again. She should be going to find Jemini so she could apologize for her behavior the previous evening. Jemini was willing to let Agnes and Kim remain in their homes and that was wonderful. She shouldn't have acted like a spoiled brat who wasn't getting her way.

Well, she wasn't getting her way. She wanted Jemini here in Riverview with her. She wanted to go home now and crawl into bed with Jemini. And to wake up every morning beside her. She rested her head against the headrest and closed her eyes. Her head was so fuzzy. Maybe food wasn't the best idea. Apparently she needed sleep more, but now they were on their way so she would eat first.

"What a night!" Jared exclaimed as he started the car.

She could only nod.

"Want to tell me about her?"

She looked at him and frowned. She had never discussed anyone she was dating with her coworkers, not that she'd ever really had any women to discuss. She considered Jared a friend.

Someone she could call if she needed to move something heavy or needed backup. Not someone with whom she'd discuss the woman she couldn't get off her mind.

"I'm really glad we could clear things up enough to release the boys to their parents," she said slowly, hoping Jared would take the hint without being offended.

"So, she's off limits, huh. Okay, but if you ever want to talk I'm here." He gave her a quick glance, and she met his eyes. "You listened to plenty of hours of me whining about Clare when we almost broke up. It would be no hardship for me to repay that friendship."

She nodded. Jared and Clare had recently set a date for their wedding and she barely remembered their short separation a year ago. She certainly couldn't take any credit for the reconciliation because all she had done was listen. Back then she didn't have any advice for someone in a long-term relationship. Now she would tell him not to give up and do everything it took to make things work. Luckily Jared had figured that out on his own.

He continued to talk. "I can't believe the boys fell for Ripkin's crap so easily. I know we're a small town, but I'm pretty disappointed in them."

She felt the same way, and she didn't know the boys like Jared did. It was surprising that someone could manipulate them so easily. She hoped Jared would be able to use this to teach other teenagers. She climbed out of the car when Jared pulled to a stop in front of the diner. They entered together, giving Vikki and Sally a wave as they chose a table in the corner.

After they placed their orders, she tried to concentrate enough to continue their conversation. "I can understand why you're disappointed. You work with them almost every day."

"Right, and I thought I had enough of a relationship that the kids would come to me if they ran into something they couldn't handle."

"Maybe you can use it as teaching experience. John did mention he thought about talking to you, but by that point they all feared for their families' safety not just their own."

"I guess Ripkin knew how to play to their fears."

Vikki set two lunch plates on their table and refilled their water glasses before disappearing without a word.

"Looks like word has spread around town already," Steph said as she watched Vikki walk away quickly.

"She just graduated last year, so I'm sure she knew all the boys involved. It's sad that our kids can't enjoy their childhood. You know, that's why I volunteered to work the position at the high school. I wanted to help make a difference in their future."

"I'm sure you have. Don't base your years working with the kids on one situation. Besides, these were fairly good kids that didn't go to their parents for help either. Unfortunately sometimes kids take advice from each other."

"Yeah, that is unfortunate."

As with every other customer in the diner, she looked up when the bell over the door sounded. Her heart raced at the sight of Jemini, and she choked on her water when Jemini started their way.

She could feel Jared's eyes on her, but she wasn't going to resist the opportunity to be close to Jemini. She slid over in the booth, making a space for her to sit.

"So this is where you hang out on a Sunday," Jemini said with a grin, her eyes slowly moving away from Steph and looking at Jared. "I'm sorry to intrude."

He reached his hand across the table. "Jared Miller."

"Jemini Rivers." She turned her focus back to Steph. "Are you still working?"

"We're finished for the moment."

"Have you been up all night?" Jemini looked back and forth at both deputies.

Steph nodded. "Do you need something?"

"I noticed the cruiser outside and was hoping to catch you. I wanted to talk with you before I meet with Mr. Cross tomorrow. I left him a voice mail about what we discussed yesterday."

"I need to go back to the station and grab my car, but then I'm free."

Jemini stood. "I'll meet you at the house then?"

"Sure, in about thirty minutes."

Jared was silent until Jemini had left the diner, but the huge grin plastered on his face was more than she was prepared for.

"So, the rumors are true. It's the newest resident of Riverview that finally turned your head," he teased.

She glared at him, giving her best shut-up stare. "I'm sure I don't know what you're talking about."

"Okay, Steph. I'll give you a break today because we've been up all night. Just so you know, though, I think it's good for you."

She shook her head. "You don't know what you're talking about." Standing, she tossed a few bills on the table. "Are you ready to go?"

He shrugged, throwing money on the table as he stood. The sunlight blinded her as she stepped out of the diner, and she quickly pulled on her sunglasses. She was surprised to see Jemini's car sitting at the curb behind their cruiser.

Jemini opened her door. "Do you want a ride? Neither of you should be behind the wheel."

Steph looked at Jared and then back at Jemini. She wanted to be with Jemini so badly, maybe too badly, but why not? Why shouldn't she spend as much time with her as she could before she left? She walked toward Jemini's car and climbed in without a word.

"Deputy Miller?" Jemini gave Jared a hard stare.

He shook his head. "I'm good. One night doesn't wipe me out." He nodded toward Steph. "She's had several in a row."

Jemini gave him a wave and climbed in the car. Steph leaned back against the headrest and closed her eyes. She felt Jemini's hand rest on her thigh as the car began to move. It felt comforting. She hoped Jemini would leave it there for the entire drive.

"Steph. Steph."

She lifted her head from the seat. Jemini stood beside her with the door open.

A hint of a smile played on Jemini's lips. "Unfortunately, I can't carry you so you're going to have to walk."

She nodded, her head heavy with sleep. She let Jemini help her from the car and leaned against her as they walked to the cottage. She pulled the keys from her pocket, and Jemini took them from her hand, opening the door. She stumbled into the bedroom and pulled off her boots. Locking her pistol inside the metal box on her dresser, she undid her belt and dropped her jeans into a pile on the floor. She knew Jemini was watching, and the fog filling her head didn't keep her from being aroused. She wanted to throw Jemini on the bed and cover her with her body. As her fingers found the buttons on her shirt, she looked up to meet Jemini's dark eyes.

Jemini crossed the room and clasped Steph's fingers, dropping them to her side. Walking her backward, Jemini moved them toward the bed until their bodies were in full contact. Steph looked down and watched Jemini slowly unbutton her shirt. Her arms felt rubbery, but she lifted them anyway and cupped Jemini's chin. She couldn't stop herself from pressing her lips gently to Jemini's. Pulling back, she studied her face and eyes, searching for resistance. She saw only arousal, and she met Jemini's lips again, pressing harder this time as she gave in to the desire to have her.

She felt Jemini's fingertips graze her breasts and her nipples hardened beneath her touch. She slid her hands under Jemini's shirt, feeling the fire of her skin. Jemini opened Steph's shirt and pushed it off her shoulders, dropping it to the floor before taking a step back and breaking their contact.

"Jemini," she groaned. "Please don't stop."

"I can't. No, you can't. Not right now." Jemini cradled Steph's head until their eyes met. "You can barely stand and as soon as you lay down you're going to be asleep."

"Then I won't lay down," Steph mumbled.

Jemini pushed her hard onto the bed. "I can only be strong for about two more seconds so I'm going to walk away now. Get under the covers and I'll check on you later."

* * *

Jemini didn't think anything could hold her attention more than the purple sports bra Steph wore until Steph whipped it off, tossing it to the floor. The glimpse she got of Steph's body was fleeting as Steph pulled the blanket over her body, but Jemini knew she would never forget the imprint of each curve. She was glad she had moved as far as the doorway before the unexpected display. She knew she shouldn't approach the bed again, but she did. She leaned down to give Steph a quick kiss good-bye, and Steph grasped her arms, pulling her closer. Steph's lips were soft and sweet like a banana the day before it's too old to eat. In this kiss was the beginning of something she had waited for her whole life. Something lasting and beautiful. She quickly retreated again. She could wait however long it took to have this opportunity. Steph's eyes were closed and the soft sounds of her breathing told Jemini she was already asleep. She backed out of the bedroom, knowing she was doing the right thing. Now if only she could convince her body of that.

The blinds in Steph's bedroom had been shut, blocking out the afternoon sun, but Jemini could still tell the walls were a light foamy sea green. The room wasn't large, and dark shadows marked the few pieces of furniture that were placed around the bed. She closed the bedroom door to block the sunlight from the living room as it spilled down the hallway. The coral color of the walls spread into a more vibrant red in the living room, making the bright and airy room feel like a beach cottage. The white plush furniture invited relaxation.

Jemini pushed through to the porch. She wanted to stay close to Steph, but she knew the temptation to return to the bedroom would be too strong. She looked out over the yard with its many small flowerbeds, bushes, and decorative trees spaced throughout. The area was perfectly balanced to highlight the variety of colors with the backdrop of the forest stretching behind. Dorothy and Steph had designed this haven, and it matched the comfort she was beginning to feel being here in their space.

As the flood of arousal in her body finally ebbed to a trickle, she folded her arms and leaned against the pillar at the edge of the porch. Her mind was at ease here. No people or work demanding her attention or her time. She thought about the moments she spent with Steph and the fire that burned through her when they were close. Steph had pushed her to feel things no one else ever had. She wanted more of this feeling. The amazing high that she couldn't seem to get enough of. There wasn't anything in Chattanooga that pulled her back. She was ready to let go of that life for a chance with Steph and a second chance to call the city of Riverview home.

She crossed to her car but couldn't convince herself to get in and leave. She might not be able to stay in the same house with Steph, but she could at least stay close by. She climbed the stairs and walked across the long front porch of Dorothy's plantation house, letting the memories flow through her. The twenty-year-old wish of never having left led to current thoughts of coming home. She unlocked the door to Dorothy's apartment and stepped inside. Walking past the pictures on the mantel, she opened all of the window blinds and let the light flood through her. She sat down at the table with her bag of Sour Cherries and a Dr. Pepper from the refrigerator and opened the box of letters again. Somewhere in these notes had to be answers to some of her questions.

She opened each one again, searching for clues that she might have missed earlier. She had spent so many years blaming Dorothy for what she had lost. Now she didn't know who to blame. Her mother for not telling her the truth? Herself for never coming back to take a chance? The things her mother had told her about what happened that fateful day were all true, but so much had changed over the years. Did her mother ever forgive Dorothy? All of the secrets she had kept made Jemini think that she hadn't, but why didn't she? Dorothy's remorse in each of the letters addressed to her was clear.

She held her head in her hands. She could forgive Dorothy, but now she had to deal with the pain of the loss she had suffered. Dorothy was gone. She would never get the chance to tell her that she forgave her or that she had never stopped loving her.

A knock on the door pulled her attention from the letters. Looking up, she was surprised to see that evening shadows had spread across the room. She walked to the door and opened it. Brandon stood on the porch and Agnes rocked in her chair nearby.

"Mom says you should stay for dinner," he announced.

She glanced at Agnes and saw the small smile on her face. Agnes continued to rock without a word. Watching her, Jemini felt a warmth spread through her body. A peaceful feeling that everything was going to be okay. She glanced down at Brandon's eager face. "I'd like that very much. Please tell your mom that I accept."

Brandon ran through the door and upstairs, his feet hitting every step.

"He's not supposed to run on the stairs," Agnes said. "We've told him he sounds like an elephant."

She was surprised to hear the kindness in Agnes's voice after their first introduction. She tentatively crossed and sat in the chair beside her. They rocked in silence with only the creaking of the chairs to connect them. Again, the warm feeling of comfort surrounded Jemini and she was surprised at how good it felt. She belonged here.

"This town grows on you, don't it?" Agnes said, breaking the silence.

"Yes, I guess it does."

"The people too. Lots of nice ones around."

"Yes."

Brandon charged back through the door. "Mom's bringing everything down to Ms. Agnes's and I'm gonna set the table."

She couldn't stop the smile as Brandon bolted back through the door. His innocent enthusiasm brightened every space he occupied. She thought about Chase, remembering the story of his last, terrifying days in foster care and how vibrant he was now. She was thankful Cassie and Kathleen had been able to bring him into their life. She seldom saw happiness in the children she represented. Their lives had been turned upside down by the time she met them, and most had developed a maturity that they would never lose.

She loved her job. Didn't she? What would she do if she moved to Riverview? Could she find a way to contribute to the town that she always believed would turn away from her? She thought about everyone she had met since she arrived. No one had treated her like the pariah she thought they might believe she was. Was it possible that Riverview was still the same town she loved as a child? It hurt to think how much she had given up because she had been afraid to take a chance on coming back. If she decided to stay, she wasn't going to miss out on anything this time.

Agnes stood. "We should help him. The last time he broke two plates and a cup. I'm running out of dishes."

She followed her through the door to the apartment across the hall from Dorothy's. A simple white door with a large B on it announced that it was a separate residence. A woman with Brandon's thick black hair and rich skin tone was coming down the stairs, and Jemini stopped to hold the door open for her. The woman's piercing black eyes were expressive as she appraised Jemini.

"Hi, I'm Kim," she said as she placed a casserole dish on the table and turned offering Jemini her hand.

"Jemini."

"It's nice to finally meet you. The whole town is buzzing with your presence, and I was starting to feel a little left out."

"Yes, this town…" She didn't know what to say. Did she love this town? Or did she hate it?

"This town can be overbearing and nosy," Agnes cut in.

"They certainly can be," Kim agreed. "But mostly they're good people."

"Where's Ms. Steph?" Brandon asked.

"She's probably working," Kim answered.

"No, she's sleeping. She worked all night again," Agnes said with a clear distaste for the hours Steph worked.

Jemini stared at the noodles cooling on her plate. Agnes seemed to know everything that went on around here, and she felt her face blush. Agnes must have seen her helping Steph into the house earlier. At least she hadn't lingered inside too long with her.

"Is she going back out tonight?" Kim asked, looking at Jemini.

"She…she didn't say," she struggled to find the words with everyone's attention focused on her.

"Well, we'll make her a plate, and you can take it over after we finish," Kim stated as if it was understood Jemini would be going over to Steph's later.

Brandon carried the conversation through dinner and she was happy to listen to his stories. She enjoyed the ones that involved Steph the most. Brandon clearly looked up to her and it was nice that she took the time to do things with him and take him places. When dinner was over, Jemini took the opportunity to tell them that she would be signing the house and the property over to Steph instead of selling it. After grilling her about remaining in Riverview, Agnes quickly left the table with Brandon to watch a baseball game on television.

She helped Kim clear the dishes from the table, and they stood side-by-side washing and drying them.

"You made us all very happy with your announcement," Kim said hesitantly. "Are you sure this is what you want? You seem sad."

She tried to smile. "It's the best option for everyone."

"And everyone includes you too?"

"I have a job and a home in Chattanooga." Why was she giving this argument again? Why didn't she want anyone to know she was thinking about what life would be like in Riverview? With every conversation she was digging herself deeper into staying in Chattanooga.

"You're a lawyer, right? You could do that anywhere."

"I could, but I worked hard to become a partner in my firm." She had everything she had always wanted, including a condo in the heart of downtown. She couldn't say it out loud, though, because she was afraid Kim would see right through her. She had everything she had always wanted, but now her wants and needs had changed.

"I won't complain about your decision. Steph is wonderful, and she'll make sure everything is handled fairly. Agnes didn't seem happy with the situation either, though."

Jemini leaned her head toward Kim and lowered her voice. "What's her deal? I thought she would be ecstatic when I told her."

Kim frowned. "I'm not sure. At least she was nice through dinner. I can't say I've seen her act like Steph described your first meeting. I bet Steph was happy when you told her, though."

"She took it about the same as Agnes, but she doesn't know I'm giving it to her. Only that I'm not going to sell it."

She could read Kim's face, and she saved her from asking. "I didn't have a chance to tell her. She got called away to work before I could."

She knew why Steph was disappointed. She was beginning to feel the same way. *I want my friend back.* She had been happy, before all of this was dropped into her lap. Now she was afraid to return to Tennessee and her lonely normal life. No friends and no Steph.

"Dishes are finished and everything is put away. Shall we see who's winning the ballgame?"

She followed Kim into the living room.

"We have to text Ms. Steph!" Brandon demanded when his mother appeared. "They won again. That's four in a row."

Yes, she thought. *Let's text Steph.* Her heart raced at the thought.

"Not while she's sleeping. You can tell her when you see her. At least she's finished with uniform patrol. I'm sure she's relieved." She looked at Jemini. "She doesn't normally work the evening shift. She's just covering for others on vacation."

"No, normally she works twenty-four hours a day," Agnes said sarcastically.

Kim shrugged. "She does work a lot, but she doesn't work a regular patrol shift."

She frowned. "She doesn't work a regular patrol shift?"

"No—"

"She's a detective," Brandon said enthusiastically, cutting his mother off.

"Brandon, it's time for bed. Let's head upstairs." Kim stood, pulling him to his feet.

Jemini was shocked when Brandon hugged her after hugging Agnes. It must have showed on her face because Kim laughed.

"He's a hugger," she explained.

"I better go too." Jemini stood. She didn't want to be left alone with Agnes. Their talk had been pleasant enough earlier on the porch, but she didn't want it to be awkward alone in Agnes's living room. She also didn't want to have another conversation about her moving to Riverview.

"Are you coming over tomorrow?" Agnes asked.

"I'm not sure." Jemini hesitated. Why did Agnes care if she was going to be around?

Agnes grunted her displeasure without looking away from the television.

Jemini glanced at Kim and they both smiled. Maybe if she hung around long enough, one day she would understand Agnes.

"We look forward to seeing you again soon," Kim said, patting her arm as they parted in the foyer.

She nodded. She looked forward to seeing them too. But no one more than Steph. She crossed the hall back into Dorothy's apartment and placed Steph's leftover dish in the refrigerator. She really wanted to go check on her, but she didn't want to wake her yet. She had told Steph she would come back, so she should hang out here for a few more hours before waking her. She leaned down and flipped on the lamp beside the couch in the living room.

* * *

Jemini's scream brought Steph quickly to her feet.

"Why are you sitting in the dark?" Jemini exclaimed, staring at her.

She rubbed her eyes as they adjusted to the light from the lamp. "I'm sorry. Your car was still here so I was waiting for you. I must have fallen asleep."

"It's okay. I didn't expect anyone to be in here. Kim sent leftovers for you. I just put them in the refrigerator."

"Great. I'm starving." Steph walked into the kitchen and pulled the container out. She needed a distraction from the closeness of Jemini. Her sleep had been filled with dreams of Jemini and her arousal was barely contained. She knew Jemini was attracted to her too, but she wasn't sure how far Jemini was willing to go. She held up the dish. "I'm going to take this back to my place. Do you want to come?"

Steph didn't want to assume anything. Jemini always seemed to push back whenever she assumed things. Asking had seemed like the right thing to do. She was still a bit surprised when Jemini nodded, no hint of hesitation in her face. Feeling the thrill of what the future might hold, Steph took Jemini's hand and together they crossed the yard.

"Do you want to go for a walk?" Steph asked when they reached her porch. She had been waiting for days to share a piece of their past with Jemini. This was the first opportunity and she didn't want to miss it.

"I thought you were starving?"

"I am, but I want to show you something. Wait here." She took her leftovers into the house and returned with a flashlight.

She was pleasantly surprised when Jemini slid her hand back into hers as they walked along the trail toward the forest. The thrill of excitement she felt at Jemini's soft touch almost sent her back toward the house. Did Jemini understand what she did to her? They hadn't talked about what was happening between them, and she knew she hadn't been clear about what she wanted from Jemini either. How could she be when Jemini had been perfectly clear about not leaving Tennessee?

"Do you have to work tonight?" Jemini asked.

"I certainly don't plan on it."

Jemini's tight squeeze of her hand sent shivers down her spine. She realized how hard she had been trying to fight this attraction and what a terrible job she had been doing. She wanted to stop fighting and follow Jemini's lead, but her heart ached at the fear of Jemini leaving again. Maybe tonight she could put away her fears and take what Jemini offered at face value. If one night was all she was offering, then that's what she would take.

* * *

Jemini clung tightly to Steph's hand. There was so much between them. Childhood memories. The attraction that was sizzling between them. And pain, so much pain that she didn't know if they would be able to move past it all. She wanted to, though. She wanted to find a way to have Steph in her life. Tomorrow she would figure out how they could make things work. Tonight she only wanted to enjoy the feel of Steph touching her.

The woods around them were dark, but she remembered running through them as a child. She had never needed a flashlight to find her way around. This was her domain. The smell of pine trees and damp leaves was all around her, and it took her breath away. As they rounded a corner on the trail, recognition hit her.

"Is our fort still here?" she asked excitedly, pushing forward on the trail and pulling Steph along. She remembered everything about the secret hiding place she and Steph had shared. The wooden panels they had borrowed from the stash Steph's father had to build his greenhouse. They had leaned the panels together and the cherished fort wasn't much more than a lean-to. In the glow from the flashlight, she could see the grin on Steph's face.

A dark shape began to rise in front of them, and Steph shined the flashlight over what was now a tiny square cabin before pushing open the door. There was just enough room inside for the small table and four little chairs. The vibrant colors on the wall were obviously left over from the renovating at Steph's cottage and they brightened in the glow from the flashlight. Four rectangle windows lined the top of each wall and Jemini could imagine what it looked like during the daylight when the sun peeked through the trees.

She gasped as she spun around the room, looking at every corner. Steph had made their special fort into every child's dream playhouse. It even had a roof and a wooden floor instead of the dirt one they had planned to have. The only thing missing was electricity and running water.

"You did everything we talked about." She took the flashlight from Steph, spinning in a circle again.

"I planned for the day you'd come back."

"I'm so sorry it wasn't sooner," she said, laying the flashlight on the table and putting her arms around Steph. She buried her face in Steph's neck and inhaled the scents. The fresh aroma from her recent shower blended perfectly with the amber smell of her cologne or body gel. The small kisses came naturally, and she didn't allow herself to think about anything but how good she felt as she made a trail of kisses to Steph's lips.

Their bodies came together in a hard embrace as their tongues met in a passionate dance. She wanted to pretend she didn't know where tonight was heading, but she did and she wanted to believe that Steph did too. She backed her into the wall and pushed hard against her, their mouths releasing and then delving back together in a rhythmic pattern. She needed to feel Steph's soft skin, and before she even realized it her fingers were grazing thin cotton-covered mounds beneath Steph's shirt. She caressed them gently, running her thumbs over both nipples.

She couldn't hold on much longer, and Steph hadn't even touched her yet. She unzipped Steph's pants and slid her hand inside. Sliding through the wetness she found there, she began a slow steady stroke. Steph's body felt like putty beneath her fingers as their bodies molded together. Her gyrating hips pushed hard into Steph's thigh. Steph's hands, which had seemed frozen on her waist, came alive with a purpose. She slid her hand inside Jemini's shorts without unfastening them. Her touch was firm and gentle and effective. Very effective. Jemini put one arm around her neck and held on tightly as convulsions racked her body.

Their kissing slowed and she struggled to hold them both upright.

"Is that lavender you're wearing?" Steph asked, inhaling deeply.

"It is. Do you like it?"

"I freakin' love it." Steph inhaled deeply again.

She shivered as Steph's expulsion of breath grazed her neck. "I really need to sit down."

"Do you think you can make it back to the cottage? I'd rather be horizontal."

Jemini nodded, enjoying the spasm that rocked Steph's body as she gently withdrew her hand from Steph's pants.

"You have to stop," Steph said, hesitating between each word.

"I'd like to apologize, but I wouldn't mean it," Jemini groaned. She took Steph's hand and grabbed the flashlight from the table, pulling her out the door.

Steph stopped as they entered her cottage. "I hope this doesn't sound too insensitive, but would you mind if I ate before we went back to bed?"

Jemini laughed. "Not at all."

"You promise you won't leave, right?"

Her laugh faded quickly as she heard the apprehension in Steph's voice. "I'm not going to leave." Jemini meant that she wouldn't leave tonight, but she couldn't help feeling like the words might mean so much more. She didn't want to leave Steph, but she also wasn't sure she knew how to stay.

She pushed Steph into a chair at the table, popped the dish into the microwave for a minute, and searched the drawers until she found silverware and a plate. As she moved around Steph's kitchen with a familiarity that surprised her, she caught Steph's eye.

"What?" she asked.

"I like you being here."

"I like being here with you," she said, placing the warmed plate of food in front of Steph.

She slipped into the chair across from her, watching her dig into the casserole. The shorter strands of hair around Steph's face had broken loose from her ponytail and she continually tucked them behind her ear as she ate. Jemini found the habitual action extremely sexy. Desire filled her again and she took a deep breath. She needed to clear things between them before they went any farther. She searched for the words to explain

She could feel her own wetness coating Jemini's thigh as she slid down her body. Several times she had to pull Jemini's hand from between them. As badly as she wanted Jemini to touch her, she needed all of her concentration. She slid between Jemini's legs and rested on her knees as she removed the last piece of clothing from Jemini's body, dropping her peach-colored panties beside the matching bra on the floor.

She layered kisses from Jemini's stomach to her inner thigh before settling between her legs. She rested her head inches from Jemini's center, letting each expulsion of breath drift across Jemini's skin.

"You're killing me here," Jemini said, her voice cracking.

Steph ran her tongue through the wetness as she lifted her head.

"Please," Jemini begged.

She spread her hand across Jemini's chest, holding her tight against the bed as she buried her head between Jemini's legs. She continued to stroke with her tongue as she sucked Jemini into her mouth. Jemini's body convulsed as she exploded, screaming Steph's name.

She rested her head on Jemini's stomach. Her body ached for another release, but at the same time she was content. She had heard Jemini call out her name and she liked it. Her mind drifted as she imagined going to sleep every night with the scent of Jemini nearby. She was just drifting off when she felt Jemini's breathing grow shallow too. For a second she considered putting her head on a pillow, but before she could put her thoughts into action she was asleep.

CHAPTER FIFTEEN

Somehow in the night, their bodies had shifted and Jemini found herself snuggled comfortably into Steph's back. She stretched her arm across Steph's stomach, and Steph stirred, pulling Jemini's hand up between her breasts. They lay quietly for several minutes before Steph spoke.

"I need to go in to work for a couple hours. Will you wait here for me?"

She raised up on one elbow and pushed Steph onto her back, looking down at her. "How can I convince you I'm not going to leave without telling you?"

Steph shrugged. "It all feels so good I keep waiting for the other shoe to drop."

"I'm not ready to leave you." She held up a finger to keep Steph from talking. "Yet. I do have some errands to do in town, however, so I'm not going to sit here all day and wait for you to come back."

"Of course." Steph grinned. "I didn't mean that. Do you want to come back here tonight, or should I come over to Lake View?"

"Why don't you call me when you finish with work? I might be back at Dorothy's by the time you finish."

"I can do that." Steph rolled to her feet. "I'm going to shower. You're welcome to join me."

"I don't think you'll make it to work if I join you."

Steph laughed and disappeared into the bathroom. Jemini swung her legs over the side of the bed and sat up. Her body was stiff and her muscles ached. She had barely convinced her legs to move again when Steph returned.

"You're fast."

Steph sent her an evil grin. "Not always."

"No, not always, but you are always bad."

Steph disappeared into the closet and returned wearing a white T-shirt and jeans. "Nah. I'm one of the good guys." She kissed Jemini. "I'll leave a key to the house on the table. Take it with you when you go and come back whenever you want."

She smiled. "Thanks. I might steal some clothes too."

"Take whatever you need."

She watched Steph clip her pistol to her jeans in the small of her back. Steph *was* one of the good guys and she felt very lucky to have her in her life. She was almost giddy with the thrill of what their future might hold.

As she disappeared, Steph called over her shoulder. "I'm not looking back at you because if I do I won't be able to leave."

She heard the front door close, and she fell back on the bed, squeezing Steph's pillow to her chest. She had a hard time believing she was back in Riverview and an even harder time believing she had just spent the night with Stephanie Williams. Over the years, she had tried to imagine what Steph had done with her life. What career she had chosen? Was there a spouse? Or kids? Nothing her mind had created could even come close to reality. Steph was a beautiful woman, and she seemed to be everything Jemini had looked for in a partner. She knew that probably wasn't completely true, but she needed to find out and the best way to do that was to move to Riverview. She could still sign everything Dorothy left her over to Steph, but doing that didn't mean she had to return to Chattanooga.

She climbed out of bed and located a set of clean sheets in the closet. After making the bed, she showered, stealing a pair of shorts and a T-shirt from Steph's closet. She piled the dirty sheets beside the washer. This afternoon she would bring back Steph's clothes and wash everything before Steph returned from work.

She drove straight to the real estate office and advised Richard to take Dorothy's house off the market. She listened politely to his begging about selling to the developer and then told him no. She stopped at Gerald Cross's office and asked his secretary to have him draw up papers transferring the property from her name to Steph's.

Back at Lake View, Jemini packed her clothes and checked out of her cabin.

"Are you leaving?" Kathleen asked when she walked into the office and found Cassie handing her a receipt for her stay.

"Do you have time for a walk?" she asked Kathleen.

"Of course."

"I'll see you later, Cassie. Thanks for everything." Jemini folded the paperwork and placed it inside her car.

Kathleen looked over her shoulder at the packed bags on the backseat of the car. "You are leaving? Did something happen?"

She grinned. "Yes, something happened. Something good." She walked toward the lake, waiting for Kathleen to fall into step beside her before continuing. "Steph and I have worked things out."

"That's good, right? Then why are you leaving?"

"Yes, it's very good. She had to work for a couple of hours, so I thought I would pack my stuff so I didn't have to wear her clothes again tomorrow."

Kathleen's eyes widened. "That's wonderful."

"I'm never going to leave," she said excitedly. "Well, that's not completely true. I have to return to Chattanooga for work and to sell my condo, but other than that I'm going to be here."

"I'm so happy." Kathleen hugged her, looking up at the house as they made a full circle. "I'd love to stay and chat, but Cassie and I have an appointment with Chase's teacher. Come to dinner tomorrow. You and Steph."

She nodded. "I'll check with Steph."

Kathleen hugged her again. "I'm so happy for you guys."

Jemini pulled her phone from her pocket and sat down on a shady bench. She had almost forgotten it was a workday. Monday mornings were always crazy at her office. She dialed in to her voice mail and was surprised to hear she had twelve messages. She walked to her car and pulled a notepad from her briefcase. Sitting in the car, she listened to each message, taking notes, her distress growing with each voice mail. Mentally preparing herself for the drive back to Chattanooga, she deleted the last voice mail and took a deep breath before placing her next call.

She dialed Steph and was disappointed when her call went straight to voice mail. She left a short message asking her to call her when she could. She didn't want to tell her she had to leave town on a voice mail. She knew she wouldn't take well the news that she was leaving. By the time she called back, however, Jemini would know more details and could tell her exactly when she would be returning.

She looked around for Kathleen or Cassie so she could reschedule tomorrow night's dinner, then remembered they had left for an appointment. Dialing Karen on the car's Bluetooth system, she pulled on the highway and headed for Tennessee.

Karen began explaining as soon as she answered. "Mr. Thompson had requested the partner meeting, but all that changed when they rushed him to the hospital last night."

"Then I'll go straight to the hospital," Jemini answered, still reeling from the news that her law partner had had a heart attack. Karen's first message had asked her to return for a meeting with her two fellow law office partners. The messages had progressed from bad to worse as Ken Thompson was rushed to the hospital and then to surgery.

"Can you go straight to the courthouse instead? I'll have Sarah meet you there with Ken's files. There's no one else to cover the hearing at three."

"Sure. Tell Sarah I'll meet her at two thirty at Duggan's. Oh, and have her bring a suit from my office." She needed coffee now, but she didn't want to take the time to stop. She'd have to wait until she met Sarah at the coffee shop. Her phone beeped again, and she looked at the readout. "Karen, I need to hang up and charge my phone. It's about to die."

"Okay. Call if anything changes. Otherwise, Sarah will see you at Duggan's."

With one hand, she searched her briefcase for her phone charger. Not finding it, she pulled to the side of road and dumped her briefcase on the seat beside her. The last time she remembered seeing it was Saturday night when she charged her phone. Was it in her bag? She opened the rear door and dumped out the bag's contents. No charger. She hurriedly shoved everything back into her bag, knowing she had to call Steph with the remaining charge left on her phone.

She climbed into the front seat and pulled back onto the highway, dialing Steph with one hand.

"Steph, I'm so sorry. I had to leave for an emergency, but I'll be back as soon as I can. My cell battery is dying and I can't find my charger, but I'll call you. I promise. I'll miss you." She spoke as rapidly as she could, but when she looked at the readout there was no display. She prayed Steph would receive her message.

* * *

Steph hadn't planned to spend the day in the courthouse, but she had been pulled in to recount her actions leading to Ripkin's arrest. His attorney was trying to get all the charges thrown out, claiming entrapment. Luckily the judge didn't seem to be buying his story. Steph listened to both of Jemini's voice mails again, trying to read any hidden message in her voice. She had sounded strained in the first message, but it was the second one that made Steph's heart hurt. No explanation and no good-bye. Just, "Steph, I'm so sorry. I had to leave."

She had felt the vibration of the calls, but she couldn't leave the judge's chambers until he called a break. It had been almost an hour since Jemini's last message, but she immediately dialed her number. She told herself not to worry when it rolled straight to voice mail. She left Jemini an apology that she missed her and asked her to call back when she could. She looked up from her phone when another deputy stepped into the hall and told her the judge was ready. She took a deep breath, sliding her phone back into her pocket, and followed the deputy back into the judge's chambers.

* * *

Jemini was pleased she was only a few minutes late for her meeting with Sarah. She took her suit and motioned Sarah to follow her to the bathroom inside Duggan's. As she dressed, Sarah briefed her on the case and which motions she needed to present in today's hearing. She passed her bag of clothes to Sarah in exchange for the court files, which she dropped into her briefcase. She took the cup of coffee Sarah handed her and began the short walk to the courthouse. Sarah stayed with her, continuing the flow of details pertaining to the case as they walked.

She borrowed Sarah's phone to call Steph, then realized Steph's number was programmed into her phone and she didn't know it by heart. Calling Karen, she asked her to contact Lake View Resort to leave a message for Kathleen that she wouldn't be able to make dinner tomorrow night. As an afterthought, she added that she was fine and would call them soon. She knew she could count on Kathleen to tell Steph that she was okay.

As they entered the courthouse, Jemini returned Sarah's phone and focused on the case in front of her. Ken's clients deserved the best she could offer.

* * *

Steph was exhausted when they finally finished in the judge's chambers. Ripkin's attorney had pushed the judge too far and in response he approved everything the sheriff's department had asked for. Search warrants had been issued and coordination was made with law enforcement agencies in Pensacola to initiate them. Ripkin's home and office were about to be ripped apart and some of his friends' homes as well. Steph's colleagues had found evidence of a theft ring that all led back to Ripkin. He would remain in their custody for now, but additional charges were pending.

She dialed Jemini again as she climbed into her truck. She left another short message for her before playing Jemini's messages again. Listening closely, she thought she heard the start of another word after Jemini said "leaving," but maybe it was her imagination or her wanting to believe Jemini wouldn't leave with just a voice mail message. She watched closely for the black Mercedes as she drove through town, hoping to find Jemini still running errands. When she didn't see her anywhere, she drove back to Rivers Pass. Jemini's car wasn't there, but Agnes greeted her from the front porch rocking chair.

"New case?"

Steph nodded, not wanting spend time talking about her work. Agnes was always supportive of her job, but she did like to harass Steph about her late nights and early mornings. She sat down beside Agnes in Dorothy's rocking chair and stared across the grassy lawn. Agnes had been right all along. Sitting in Dorothy's chair was okay. Sitting in her chair didn't mean she was forgotten. She took a deep breath and braced herself for Agnes's teasing. "Have you seen Jemini today?" she asked, trying to keep her voice casual.

"Not since she left your house this morning."

She knew she was too old to blush, but she felt her face grow warm anyway. She took a quick glance at Agnes and saw the smile on her face growing bigger. She couldn't hold back her own smile, but then she remembered the messages from Jemini. She didn't know what to feel. She had trusted her when she said she wouldn't leave, but now she had left and Steph wasn't sure what she was supposed to do. Asking for advice from Agnes didn't seem like a good idea.

"Okay. If she comes by ask her to call me."

"Going back to work?"

She didn't want to lie to Agnes, but she also didn't want to tell her that she might have screwed things up with Jemini. Again. The smile on Agnes's face was the first real one she had seen there since Dorothy had passed away, and she didn't want to be responsible for it disappearing again.

"I have to run some errands. I'll be back in an hour or so."

"Okay. I'll keep watch for your girl."

She didn't correct Agnes because she liked the sound of Jemini being her girl. She dialed Jemini's phone again as soon as she got in her truck. This time she didn't leave a message. She forced herself to drive slowly back through Riverview and then turned into Lake View. Steph pushed away her disappointment when she saw Jemini's car wasn't there either. She sat in her truck staring at the lake. She wasn't sure she was ready to hear what Cassie and Kathleen had to say.

Two children played quietly on the beach while their parents watched nearby. It was a tranquil scene and she used it to help calm herself. She wanted to believe Jemini wouldn't leave for good without telling her. She had to believe that after the night they had shared. Touching her had been amazing and she had slept so peacefully. Jemini seemed to fit perfectly into her home and life. She wasn't ready to give up on what was only just beginning. Finally, she slid out of her truck and climbed the steps into the Lake View Resort office.

Dillon Varner and his wife, Shelley, were sitting at the desk with their heads leaned together. Dillon was the resort's go-to guy for all things farming and Shelley helped out at the desk a few hours a week. Both were in their early thirties with no children yet and seemed to live at the resort. She thought maybe she had heard Cassie mention that they were going to build a house on the resort property. She liked them both a lot.

"Have either of you seen Jemini Rivers today?" she asked as soon as they looked up at her.

"Nope," Dillon said as he passed Steph and headed out the front door. "Good to see you and I'd love to chat, but I got horses to tend to."

She had spent a lot of time around Dillon and Shelley when she was at the resort interviewing Chase. She had followed the boy around while he did his chores, letting him relax and tell her in his own words what had taken place the night his foster parent was murdered. Dillon was a sweet man and was always willing to help, but she'd noticed that he seemed to have a sixth sense about when emotions and feelings were about to be shared. If at all possible, he would head for the horses to get away from it. She could tell by his reaction that either her question or her appearance was revealing more than she intended.

Shelley on the other hand was a pit bull. If she thought something was wrong and that she could possibly help, she would drag it out of you. She'd go for not only the problem you might be facing but how it made you feel. Every little hidden emotional response or feeling. She steadied herself for Shelley's inquisition.

"You look upset." Shelley's eyes narrowed. "Is everything okay?"

"It's fine. I got a message to call Jemini, but I haven't been able to reach her. I was hoping to track her down here." She forced her voice to sound normal without showing the panic she was starting to feel.

"I haven't seen her, but I know she checked out today. Kathleen made a note to clean her cabin."

The office phone rang, and Shelley apologized before picking it up. Steph couldn't help but be relieved that maybe she was going to escape baring her soul to Shelley. Shelley jotted down a note as she hung up the phone.

"That was Karen, Jemini's assistant. Apparently, Jemini had made plans to have dinner here tomorrow night, and Karen was calling to cancel them."

She quickly backed toward the door. "Okay. Thanks, Shelley."

She had to get out of there fast. It was clear Jemini had left, and she could already see the pity on Shelley's face. She couldn't stay another minute or answer a single question. She sat in the truck for several minutes before pulling out. She wasn't sure what to do now. She didn't know why Jemini had left or if she was coming back, but for her own sanity she wanted to believe she was.

She drove past the iron trestle bridge and almost stopped. It held so many memories but none more prevalent than finding

Jemini there in the fading sunlight just the other night, her dark hair blowing in the gentle breeze. She would never forget their kiss that night—or any of their kisses for that matter. Jemini's body language had told her more than her words ever had. Jemini cared about her—she didn't doubt that—but did she care enough to give up her life in Chattanooga or even to attempt a long-distance relationship? Her mind swirled with thoughts of the potential of a life they could have together or what her life might be like if Jemini didn't come back. She remembered the pain Jemini had caused her thirteen-year-old self to suffer. The one place that had brought her comfort that day had been Dorothy's house, where, curled up on the big sofa with Dorothy nearby, she had cried for days.

She headed back there now, slowing her truck as she turned onto Rivers Pass and letting herself imagine that Jemini's car would be in the driveway. It was crushing to find that it wasn't, but she climbed the steps anyway, unlocking the door to Dorothy's house. Other than the few times she had been in here with Jemini, she hadn't been inside since Dorothy had passed away. She walked through the living room, running her hand along the furniture and the walls as she looked at everything as if for the first time. Dorothy had been tidy and didn't allow clutter to fill her house. The few pictures she had displayed had been there for years. Steph had stopped looking at them years ago, but now she stared at little Jemini and thought about how things might have been different if only Dorothy hadn't responded to Jemini's mother the way she did.

The box of letters was still sitting out. Steph carried it into the kitchen. She pushed the bag of candy and open bottle of Dr. Pepper to the side, making room on the table before dumping the letters out. A part of her felt like she was invading Jemini's privacy, but she wanted to try to see the pain that Jemini had known. She opened the oldest letter and began to read.

CHAPTER SIXTEEN

Jemini stepped quietly into Ken's hospital room. He was alone and appeared to be sleeping. She sat down in the wooden chair by the window and watched him. Ken had been more of a father to her than her father had ever been. She wasn't sure when she had caught his attention, but she certainly knew why. Ken's wife, Jean, had met her mother on a quiet Christmas morning at the diner where Aries worked when they first arrived in Chattanooga. Jean had convinced the single mother to share her story and then visited her on a weekly basis until she was able to find her a better job. Aries had worked at the non-profit organization that Jean started until the day she had died. It was an immediate friendship that had only grown with time.

To her, it felt like Ken and Jean had always been around. They had attended her high school graduation and encouraged her to keep on the path to becoming an attorney. Along with her mother, they were the only family she had in the audience when she graduated with her four-year degree. Ken had even hired her to work in his law office during the summers. When she passed the bar on her first try, Jean wanted her to join Ken's firm, but Jemini wanted a chance to prove herself as a formidable attorney first. Ken had waited patiently while she tried her hand in the prosecutor's office and then as a defense attorney.

Jean's guidance had led her into child advocacy, which had opened the door quicker than expected to the partnership with Ken and Keith. It was one of the few areas that they had not focused their careers in and it became her baby, her life even. Ken had always been honest and fair with her, never pushing her to make choices he wanted but leading her into making decisions that were best for her. When her mother had passed away, Ken and Jean had stood by her side at the viewing and the funeral. He had consulted with her every day on her cases until she was ready to return. He never demanded anything of her, but in his quiet way he pulled the best from her.

Karen had given her the medical update when she called her earlier. He was going to be okay, although it had been a little scary until he had the surgery. He would need to take it easy and cut back on his office hours according to what Jean had told Karen. Poor Jean. Jemini could only imagine how scared she was.

She shook her head. Now was not the time for her to ask for a leave of absence. She needed to help carry the firm that had her name in the title too. Time wouldn't be her friend over the next couple of months. She would have to help Keith carry Ken's cases as well as the ones she already carried. She would have to work hard to make Steph understand she wasn't pulling away from her. Her hearted ached at desiring to be with her but knowing she wouldn't be able to give her the attention she deserved.

She stood and turned to leave. She needed to talk with Keith so they could develop a plan for the future.

"Jemini?" Ken's voice was hoarse.

She turned and walked back to the side of his bed. "How are you?"

"I'm feeling better now that the surgery is over. Who knew that tingling in my arm all these years was a blockage?"

"Didn't it bother you?"

"Only when it affected my golf swing," he joked, but then grew serious. "The doctors say I'm going to be good as new."

"That's great. I'm sorry I wasn't here."

"It's fine. Keith said you took care of my hearing today. Thank you."

"Keith and I will handle the office. You work on getting better."

He patted her hand. "That's kind of you, but you have enough going on with your family in Florida. That's part of the reason I called the meeting on Friday. We need to talk about the future."

"Really, Ken, can't it all wait until you're back in the office?"

"I don't believe in putting anything off anymore. Time is too short. Besides we're all here now."

She turned and smiled at Keith as he walked into the room. He gave her a quick kiss on the cheek before pulling up another chair and motioning her to take a seat.

"How are you feeling, Ken?" Keith asked.

"Good. Ready to get things settled between all of us."

Jemini looked back and forth between them. "I've only been gone four days. What did I miss?"

"Ken came to see me on Friday when he found out about the blockage. They'd scheduled him for surgery this week, and I think he might've been a little concerned about his longevity."

Ken cut him off. "No, I'd been thinking about this for a while. I want to retire. I'd like to give my seat in the partnership to my son. If that's agreeable to both of you."

"That's certainly fine with me." Jemini looked at both of them. It was now or never. She deserved to be happy and Steph made her happy. Being back in Chattanooga made her heart race and her blood pressure spike, but it wasn't in a good way. Not like when she was with Steph. She was tired of the rushed lifestyle where something or someone demanded every second of her time. She wanted what Kathleen and Cassie had. Something to enjoy every day and someone to share her life with. She took a deep breath and blurted out, "While we're making changes, I'd like to leave the partnership."

"I was afraid you might want to do that. I know going home and reconnecting with your family wasn't what you ever thought you wanted," Ken said. "But I talked to Karen after you were here on Friday and I could see that things had changed for you. If you're sure about leaving, Keith and I will buy you out."

Keith nodded his agreement.

"I'll travel back and forth until all my open cases are closed, but I won't take any new ones." She smiled at both of them as her eyes filled with tears. "I'm going to miss you guys."

"We'll work out the details over the next couple of weeks while you're closing your cases," Keith suggested. "Will you be in the office tomorrow?"

"Not unless you need me. I had to leave Riverview without telling anyone where I was going and my cell phone battery is dead again."

"Go, Jemini, but don't be a stranger." Ken patted her hand. "Thank you for coming."

"I'll walk you out." Keith patted Ken's leg. "I'll come back in a minute."

They walked in silence to the elevator and Keith punched the button. "Are you okay?" he asked, giving her shoulders a squeeze.

"I am. Are you?"

He shook his head. "I'm not sure. It was an eye-opener for both of us, that's for sure. If I had a wife at home, I'd probably retire too, but I'm certainly going to look at life a little differently. I'm just really glad he's been given a second chance."

"What about the practice? I feel like we're all walking out on you at once."

"Ken won't go away easily, but I'll make sure his workload is greatly reduced." He hugged her. "We'll miss you, though. I might have to bring in another woman as partner to keep us on our toes the way you did."

She laughed. "I can recommend a few people."

"That would be good," he said, stepping back as the doors to the elevator opened and she stepped inside. "Take care of yourself, Jemini."

"I will. You too, okay? I'll call and let you know when I'll be back so we can discuss everything. And, please let me know if you need my help with any of Ken's cases."

She leaned her head against the wall as the doors closed. She was relieved Ken was going to be okay. Keith would become senior partner and he would enjoy it. He was divorced, but his daughter had two children. He had never played an active role in their lives, but she had a feeling all that would change now.

It was going to be hard to leave, but she was looking forward to telling Steph she had made one step toward moving to Riverview. *Oh no! Steph!* She needed to get to her condo to charge her phone. She hoped Steph had received her message and wasn't worried.

The doors opened and Robin stepped into the elevator.

"You're back," she said happily. "Were you looking for me?"

"No, not really. Ken had a heart attack."

"Oh, wow. Is he okay?"

She nodded. "He is now."

"So you're headed back to Podunk?"

She tried not to be irritated with Robin's bashing of Riverview. She knew some people would never understand the draw of a small town. She almost laughed. She had been one of those people, and now she couldn't wait to get back there. "I'm moving there."

Robin's eyes widened. "Are you selling your condo?"

"Yes." She saw the eagerness in Robin's eyes. "Are you interested?"

"Absolutely. Draw up the papers. Can I leave my stuff for now?"

She nodded. "Sure, in fact go ahead and move in. I'll take a few things with me tonight and have the movers come by next week. Do you want the furniture?"

"Don't you want it?"

"I already have everything I need." It hit her how real that statement was. Whether she stayed at Lake View, Dorothy's, or moved in with Steph, she really did have everything she needed. Steph made her life complete.

"Sure, leave whatever you want."

The elevator doors opened and she stepped out into the night air without looking back. She felt like a huge weight had been lifted off her shoulders. She knew Robin and others that knew her would never understand what she had just done, but she didn't care. Her life was about to become everything she had always wanted, and now she had another piece of good news to share with Steph. She drove straight to her condo and loaded her trunk with clothes and a few personal items. As soon as she was in her car, she plugged in her cell phone. Her first call was to Karen to see if she could meet her on her way out of town. She had one more thing to take care of in Chattanooga, and then she could tell Steph she was coming home to her.

* * *

Steph rubbed her face and popped another Cherry Sour into her mouth. She shivered at the tart taste as she did every time she crushed the little balls with her teeth. She read the final letter Dorothy had sent to Jemini again. It was almost like Dorothy knew she was running out of time. It wasn't like the other letters. This one begged for Jemini's forgiveness and asked her to consider giving Riverview another chance. Not to give her another chance, Steph noted, but for Jemini to visit Riverview and to consider what the town had to offer. She picked up her phone and dialed Jemini again. As had been the case all evening, voice mail picked up on the first ring. She wanted to leave another message, but what else could she say? Irritated that Jemini wouldn't answer and at herself for continuing to call, she tossed her phone on the table.

She wouldn't allow herself to pursue Jemini any farther, even though she wanted to. She had spent countless hours today recalling the events of last night. She had been looking forward to spending many more evenings with Jemini, but it clearly wasn't meant to be. If Jemini wasn't ready for a relationship or had felt the need to run, then Steph wasn't going to chase her down. Jemini had to come back on her own.

A flash of light outside the window caught Steph's eye, and she stood quickly, flipping off the lamp. Her eyes followed the beam of light and she was glad to have her pistol still resting in the small of her back. She quietly opened the front door and walked down the steps, moving toward the flashlight. The closer she got the clearer the voices became and the angrier she was.

"Two steps to your right," a male voice said.

"Yep, right there," another male voice said, but this one she recognized.

She heard a hammer pounding on wood and she quickly walked toward them. "Richard, what the hell are you doing?" she demanded, confronting the real estate agent.

"I'm…we're…I have every right to be out here."

She shook her head. "You might have permission to be on the property but not to sneak around after dark."

Her anger soared even higher as she saw the property stakes Richard carried. She fought to rein it in before she pummeled Richard for his stupidity.

"Ms. Rivers is going to want to hear what Cliff has to say." He motioned at the man with him. "He's raising his offer. She won't be able to refuse now and you should hear what he has to say as well, since he'd like to buy your house too."

"Richard, I'm going to ask you nicely to leave. If Cliff has a legitimate offer for Ms. Rivers, he can make it tomorrow during daylight hours, but I'm telling you right now I will *not* be selling."

She appreciated that Cliff had remained silent, and she watched them traipse back through the trees toward the road. Apparently they hadn't even pulled into the driveway, which explained why she didn't see them arrive. She followed them until she heard the car start and pull away.

Her anger was beyond the boiling point as she walked back to Dorothy's and locked the front door. Apparently Jemini had given Richard permission to survey the property and everything she had said about not selling had all been a hoax. One big lawyer lie. She couldn't think of a reason for Jemini to deceive her, but with her not answering her phone, it was getting harder and harder to make excuses for her. She wanted answers and she wanted them now. Jemini needed to explain why she ran and why she gave Richard permission to survey the property if she wasn't going to sell.

She climbed in her truck and began to drive. The farther she got from Riverview the crazier she realized this was. She didn't know how to find Jemini in Chattanooga. She did have the address for Jemini's law practice, but by sitting in the parking lot all night until they opened in the morning she would only embarrass herself. Confronting Jemini at her practice was not what she wanted either. She was thinking about calling Cassie to help her organize her thoughts when she realized Jemini must have used her home address when she checked in at Lake View.

She reached for her phone to call Cassie. It wasn't in her front pocket. That's when she remembered tossing it on the table in Dorothy's house. She pulled off the road and leaned her head against the steering wheel. Sometime in the last several days, she had fallen in love with Jemini and lost her mind, not necessarily in that order. She didn't go anywhere without her phone and now she was driving to Tennessee without it and in possession of a concealed weapon.

First things first. She needed to tell Jemini how she felt. She pulled back on the road until she reached the next convenience store where she bought a throwaway cell phone.

She dialed Cassie. She was prepared to leave a message since she didn't think Cassie would answer her phone this late, especially one from an unknown number.

"Hello."

She could hear the annoyance in Cassie's voice, but she pushed forward. "Cassie, it's Steph. I'm very sorry to call this late but I need a favor."

"Okay."

"Do you have Jemini's home address?"

"What's going on?"

"I'm not sure. She's avoiding my calls, and I just found Richard traipsing around in the dark marking the property lines at Dorothy's place."

"Where are you?"

Steph hesitated. "I'm on my way to Chattanooga."

"Tennessee? Hold on."

Steph could hear Kathleen talking in the background as Cassie explained the situation to her.

"Steph."

"Hey, Kathleen." She braced herself for Kathleen to begin the scolding for her stupidity.

"We have Jemini's address. I remember checking her in. Just give me a minute to get to the office and I'll get it for you."

She waited silently, pulling a pen and paper from her glove box.

Kathleen read off the address.

"Thanks, Kathleen."

"I spoke with her this morning when she checked out and she was really happy. I'm not sure what's going on, but I can't imagine that she's running from you."

"You don't think I'm crazy?"

"Not crazy, but maybe in love."

"I'm not ready to say that out loud yet."

Kathleen laughed. "You have the rest of your drive to get to that point, and you better be prepared to speak since you are making the drive."

"I hear you."

"Call us when you get back."

"Thanks again."

She typed Jemini's address into her truck's GPS system and pulled back out on the road. She had two hours to decide what she wanted to say to Jemini. Would she be able to tell her that she loved her? She wanted to, but she couldn't be sure if Jemini would want to hear it.

CHAPTER SEVENTEEN

Jemini dialed Steph's number and listened to the line ring before voice mail kicked in. Apparently it wasn't turned off anymore, but now Steph wasn't answering. She was definitely driving back to Riverview after she met with Karen. She had to see Steph and make sure everything was okay between them. She climbed out of her car and met Karen at the door of the restaurant. The smell of fresh baked bread and melting cheese assaulted her when she walked in the door and she decided very quickly she needed more than coffee. She couldn't remember the last time she had eaten.

They were seated in a dark blue plastic booth, and she was thankful she had taken the time after leaving the hospital to change back into jeans. Even through the denim she could feel the cold of the plastic bench. Although the temperature outside had cooled from the heat of the day, the diner appeared to still have the air conditioner on. She picked up the menu, and her eyes found the source of the wonderful smell that filled the room. Today's special was grilled cheese and tomato sandwich on fresh sourdough bread.

The waiter, a college student, bounced between tables and his open course books on the counter. His blond hair was thick with hair gel, making it stand up in the front. The thin strand of hair above his lip contradicted his pudgy baby face and his smile was contagious. He was attentive and quick, returning with their drinks before he took their food orders.

"Is Ken retiring?" Karen asked as soon as she ordered today's special too.

Karen had dropped the formalities years ago when she was alone with Jemini, but she would respectfully revert to Mr. Thompson and Mr. Myers if anyone else was present.

"Officially he is, but he's probably still going to be around for a while. His son is going to join the firm too."

"He's been around a lot lately and everyone likes him so that won't be a hardship." Karen's eyes studied Jemini. "Will I still be there?"

"That'll be up to you. I told them I'm leaving. I'll travel back and forth until all of my cases are closed, but I won't take anything new."

"You plan to open a practice in Riverview?"

She leaned back as their food was placed on the table. Was she going to take the Florida state bar and open a firm in Riverview? She hadn't really given it much thought, but of course she would. She would probably have to return to general practice since the need for a child advocate in a small town probably wasn't enough to support her and Karen both. In Chattanooga, she had been available anytime night or day, and she wasn't sure what she would want now. She needed to talk with Steph before she made too many decisions. One thing was definite, though: she was moving to Riverview.

"Yes, I'll be opening an office. I just don't know what I'll be doing yet. Have you thought about coming with me?"

Karen cut her sandwich in half and took several bites before speaking. "I want to go with you."

She smiled. Having Karen along for the ride certainly made things easier for her. "I'm glad to hear you say that, but come for a visit first. Make sure it's really a place you could call home."

"Okay, but I'm ready for a change. I haven't planted a flower in almost twenty years. Or even looked out my window at a blade of grass. I'm tired of concrete and asphalt."

"I'll need you to stay here until all of my cases close. Maybe six months or even a year."

"You'll be driving back and forth?"

"I will. Robin's going to buy my condo, so I'll need to move out right away. I'll get a hotel room if I need to stay more than a day at a time."

She could see Karen was struggling with something she wanted to say. It was odd to see her at a loss for words, and she always valued Karen's perspective. She encouraged her to speak her mind whenever possible. "What's bothering you?"

Karen pushed her half-eaten sandwich away and stared into her caramel-colored coffee. "Why now? Why move there after your grandmother has passed away?"

She wasn't sure how much information Karen needed or even wanted, but she knew she was trying to understand. She could certainly see how crazy it all would look to someone on the outside.

She waited for Karen to meet her eyes before answering. "My grandmother forced my mother to leave, but later she had a change of heart. Unfortunately I didn't know that until this week."

"Would you have gone back if you knew that before she died?"

She took a deep breath. Karen always asked the hard questions. Yes. The answer was a definite yes. She would have made the trip to see Dorothy. Clearly her mother wasn't able to forgive Dorothy's words or actions, but she did. Dorothy had deserved a second chance, and she probably would have given her one. In any case, she truly believed she could leave all of that in the past now. Riverview was where Steph lived and she wanted—no, she needed—to be where Steph was. It was time to come clean with Karen.

"I met someone. Well, I got reacquainted with someone I knew years ago."

Karen narrowed her eyes. "Please tell me that you aren't turning your life upside down for a woman. And one that you barely know."

Jemini smiled. "It's not like that."

"Not like Robin? Here for now and gone on a whim."

"She's nothing like Robin. She's very special to me and I need to be close to her. I want this more than anything I've ever wanted in my life."

"And she feels the same way?"

Again Karen dug into the crevice of doubt in her mind. What was Steph thinking? It was clear that Steph didn't want her to leave. Didn't that say everything she needed to hear?

"I believe she does, but I'm not going to speak for her. We've barely had any time to talk about the future. Let's forget I mentioned that. The town of Riverview is quaint with a grassy circle right in the middle of town. Things move slower there, and it doesn't take long for the people to grow on you."

Karen shook her head. "I don't think I've ever seen this side of you. Impulsive is not a word I would use to describe you. I can't wait to see this town. And this woman."

"Why don't you come down Friday after work? I'll reserve you a cabin at the resort. They have a cookout every Friday, and you'll be able to meet my friends. Then on Saturday I'll show you around."

"Sounds like a plan. Are you headed back tonight?"

"Yes," she said without hesitation, standing. "Right now." She needed to see Steph. She didn't want to think that anything was wrong between them, but she needed to make sure Steph knew why she had left with only a voice mail.

She paid the bill and gave Karen a hug before climbing into her car. The lights of Chattanooga disappeared in her rearview mirror as she turned south following Interstate 59. This was the third time in a week that she had made this drive to Riverview, but this time felt different. Her mother had taught her at a young age to be cautious about love, and now for the first time in her life she was listening to her heart. She was going home.

* * *

Steph watched the lights of Chattanooga grow closer as she followed the mechanical GPS voice toward Jemini's condominium. It was almost midnight and for the billionth time in the last few hours, she wished she had her phone so she could call her. Had she been thinking when she spoke to Kathleen earlier, she would have asked for Jemini's number as well as her address. Jemini probably wouldn't answer an unknown number so late, but she could have left her a message. She certainly could not call Kathleen again.

She maneuvered her truck through the city streets, pulling into a parking garage below Jemini's condo. She parked in visitor parking and signed in at the empty desk, giving Jemini's condominium number. She thought about waiting for the security guard to return so she could call first, but she didn't know how long that would take. She was here now, and she wanted to see Jemini. She crossed to the elevators and pressed the up button.

She could hear the music coming from Jemini's condominium as soon as the elevator doors opened. She couldn't believe the neighbors were tolerating this. She hesitated at the door. Jemini didn't seem like the kind of person who would disrespect her neighbors especially at this hour. Well, at least she knew Jemini was awake.

She had to knock several times before the door was opened. A woman with spiked black hair opened the door, releasing the barrage of sound. She could see several people behind her but not Jemini, and no one seemed interested in her.

"I'm looking for Jemini Rivers."

The woman shook her head and leaned seductively against the door. "She's not here, but maybe I can help you."

"Do you know when she'll be back?"

"I'll ask Robin. She lives here."

The woman disappeared to find Robin, but Steph didn't wait. She'd heard enough. Robin lived here in Jemini's condo. Jemini had never mentioned that there was anyone in her life, but she shouldn't be surprised. At that moment, she realized that she had never asked. Maybe because she was afraid of the answer. How stupid was she? Sure, Jemini and Robin could be roommates, but she wasn't going to wait around and ask. She was already humiliated enough. It had been a stupid idea to drive here. Jemini had never mentioned anything about her life here and now she knew why. She had driven all this way to talk to her, but now she didn't even want to see her. She climbed in her truck and headed back to Riverview.

* * *

Disappointed that Steph's truck wasn't in the driveway, Jemini unlocked Dorothy's house and went inside. She didn't know if Agnes was a light sleeper so she tried to be as quiet as possible. She had tried to call Steph several times during her drive, but her phone continued to ring and then pass to voice mail. Steph's phone was on, but she was choosing to not answer it. She would leave her a message to let her know she was at Dorothy's. If Steph wanted to see her when she finished at work, then she could come here.

She dialed the number one last time and jumped at the ringing phone behind her. Steph's phone lay on the kitchen table surrounded by little red balls of candy. She couldn't believe she had gone to work without it. Surely as soon as she realized she didn't have it, she would return for it, even if she wasn't finished working yet. Jemini slid her phone back into her pocket and carried Steph's phone onto the porch. She sat down in one of the rockers to wait for Steph.

She saw the lights on the road before they even turned in Rivers Pass and she stood. She wanted to race across the driveway and throw herself into Steph's arms, but she made herself wait patiently on the porch.

Steph parked beside her car but seemed to hesitate as she climbed out. Jemini couldn't read her face in the dark so she waited until Steph was beside her before talking. "Did you get my message?"

"Yes."

"I'm sorry it took so long for me to get my phone charged."

Steph's mouth twitched in a slight smile. "Your battery died again?"

She nodded. "And I went to the hospital before picking up my charger."

"Hospital?"

"One of my law partners had a heart attack, but he's going to be fine. That's why I had to leave so quickly."

Jemini could see relief in Steph's face. "I tried to call you once I got it charged, though." She held up Steph's phone.

"I got distracted and then left in a hurry." Steph took the phone and slipped it into her pocket.

"Distracted?"

"Richard was here marking the property line with the developer."

"What!" she exclaimed. "I specifically told him to take the property off the market."

"You did?"

"Of course I did. I'm transferring everything to you."

"Oh."

The disappointment in Steph's voice tore through her, and she wanted to fall into her arms. First she needed to tell Steph all the good news she had. "I'm staying though. If you're ready to rent out Dorothy's half."

"What about everything you have in Tennessee?" Steph hesitated again. "And Robin?"

Robin? How does Steph know about Robin? "What about Robin?"

"I met her tonight. Well, almost met her. I left before she came out."

She was really confused. Why would Robin come here looking for her? It must have had something to do with the condo, but why wouldn't she call first. "Robin was here?"

"No, when I got your message that you were leaving, I drove to Chattanooga to talk you into coming back. Robin was having a party at your condo."

"What?" *Robin was having a party?* She shook her head. She didn't care about Robin or her condo anymore. "I wasn't leaving you. I didn't leave you. I left Riverview because Ken had a heart attack, and I needed to check on him."

Steph rubbed her face. "It seemed like you were still talking when the message cut off, but all I got was you were sorry you had to leave. It seemed pretty final."

"And then you couldn't reach me." She slid her arms around Steph's waist. "I'm so sorry, but I can't believe you drove all the way to Chattanooga."

"I couldn't understand what had happened after we parted yesterday, and even Kathleen said you were happy when she talked to you. Then when Richard showed up..." Steph shrugged. "I kind of lost it. I wanted to see your face if you were telling me it was over."

She silenced Steph's words with a kiss, and Steph instantly deepened it. Jemini pulled her closer, savoring the connection that hadn't been lost between them.

Steph pulled away and took a step backward. "What about Robin?"

"I was dating Robin, but I ended things with her on Friday before the cookout." She held up her hand before Steph could ask more. "She's going to buy my condo, and I told her she could move in. I just didn't know she would do it today."

"You're selling your condo? What about your partnership?"

"I'm selling my condo, and I won't be taking any new cases in Chattanooga. I'll have to travel back and forth for a while, but after that you'll be stuck with me."

Jemini could see the happiness on Steph's face before she pulled her close again.

Steph's voice vibrated through her body as she buried her head in Steph's neck.

"I'm happy to be stuck with you. I can't believe how fast everything got so confused. From now on I'm going to make sure you have a phone charger in your car."

"I should probably tell you that I'm bringing a woman with me when I move my practice here. Just so there's no confusion— her name is Karen and she is my assistant. There is nothing between us and there never has been."

Steph smiled. "I'm glad we cleared that up."

"Me too." Agnes's voice drifted from the open window on the porch.

"Go to bed, Agnes," Steph called.

"She's finally home," they heard Agnes say as she disappeared from the window.

Steph chuckled before leaning in for another kiss. "She's been talking about you coming home for days now."

"I feel like I'm home."

"And I got my friend back."

She leaned against Steph as they walked toward the cottage. Listening to her heart had never been so sweet.

Bella Books, Inc.

Women. Books. Even Better Together.

P.O. Box 10543
Tallahassee, FL 32302

Phone: 800-729-4992
www.bellabooks.com